STOLEN KISSES FROM A ROCK STAR

RICH AND FAMOUS SERIES

CHERRY
BLOSSOM
ROMANCE

STOLEN KISSES FROM A Rock Star

JUDY CORRY

Stolen Kisses from a Rock Star

Also By Judy Corry

Rich and Famous Series:

Assisting My Brother's Best Friend (Kate and Drew)

Hollywood and Ivy (Ivy and Justin)

Her Football Star Ex (Emerson and Vincent)

Friend Zone to End Zone (Arianna and Cole)

Stolen Kisses from a Rock Star (Maya and Landon)

Eden Falls Academy Series:

The Charade (Ava and Carter)

The Facade (Cambrielle and Mack)

The Ruse (Elyse and Asher)

The Confidant (Scarlett and Hunter)

The Confession — (Nash and Kiara) — Coming 2023!

Ridgewater High Series:

When We Began (Cassie and Liam)

Meet Me There (Ashlyn and Luke)

Don't Forget Me (Eliana and Jess)

It Was Always You (Lexi and Noah)

My Second Chance (Juliette and Easton)

My Mistletoe Mix-Up (Raven and Logan)

Forever Yours (Alyssa and Jace)

Standalone YA

Protect My Heart (Emma and Arie)

Kissing The Boy Next Door (Lauren and Wes)

For my parents.

Thank you for always being there for me and teaching me the value of hard work.

Also, thanks for stepping in and saving the day when we needed it during the crazy of homeschool during COVID-19 quarantine. This story would not have gotten written without you.

CHAPTER ONE

"WE BETTER NOT SEE ANYONE I know while we're here," I said when I walked out of the women's restroom at Basset's House of Jump wearing a hideous pair of orange gym shorts that who knows how many people had worn previously.

For some reason, when I told my best friend Emma that I'd meet her here after closing my floral shop for the day, I hadn't even considered that the facility wouldn't allow me to jump in my jeans.

"You don't look so bad." Emma eyed me as she stood there looking amazing in the black yoga pants and tank top from her new fitness clothing line.

I looked down at the bright orange shorts that I was practically drowning in since they were made for a man several inches taller than a five-foot-three-inch woman like myself. "Let's just hope we don't run into anyone we recognize while we're here."

It had to be possible, right? We might be in our hometown of Maplebridge but there couldn't be that many people our age jumping at this place on a Friday evening.

"Are you excited to jump?" Piper, Emma's six-year-old daughter, asked me from beside her mother.

And I couldn't help but smile at the little cutie in her pink tank and leggings that matched her mom's, because she was adorable.

"I am excited to jump, Miss Piper," I said, putting my hands on my hips. "But are *you* excited?"

Piper nodded and smiled a big toothy grin that showed the gap where her two front teeth had been this winter. "It's going to be the funnest day ever."

"Yes, it will!" I said, loving her enthusiasm.

I may be about eight years behind Emma in the getting-married-and-having-babies department, but I did love her kids. She and her husband Arie had been together since we graduated high school ten years ago, and they really did make the cutest babies together what with their dark hair, striking blue eyes, and olive complected skin.

Piper turned to her mom, tugging on her hand. "Can we go inside now? We're going to miss it."

Emma smiled patiently at Piper. "We'll go in as soon as your daddy and Blair get back from the bathroom, okay?"

Blair was their four-year-old who had been doing the potty dance while we were standing in line for our wristbands.

Piper looked like she was about to complain about her sister taking too long in the bathroom when Arie and Blair appeared on the other side of the room. And a minute later, we were entering the gym area and stowing our shoes in the shoe bins the facility kept near the entrance.

"Where should we go first?" Emma asked me after Arie took the girls to the kids' area.

"I'm not sure," I said, surveying the room full of trampolines. "I've never been to a place like this before."

There were a few trampolines with basketball hoops along the back wall. An obstacle course was on the right. The kids' area was to the left.

But right in front of us was the trapeze swing where kids and teens were swinging into a pit full of green and black foam squares.

I'd always wondered what it would feel like to land in a huge pile of foam cubes. I imagined it was probably a lot like landing on a big cloud.

"Do you want to try that?" I pointed at the trapeze, deciding it looked the most fun.

"Sure." Emma shrugged. "It's your birthday weekend. I'll go anywhere you want."

So we got in line, and I tried not to feel completely out of place in my baggy shorts among all the kids.

Despite feeling like the odd woman out, as I watched the kids swing and drop into the pit ahead, my anticipation grew. I may be a childless, single woman about to turn twenty-eight tomorrow—which by Utah standards basically meant I was an ancient old maid—but standing there and waiting for my turn with my best friend since kindergarten made me feel like a kid again.

A girl at the front of the line, who had to be about ten, grabbed the trapeze and swung herself into the foam pit, landing gracefully before climbing out.

"Do you want to go first? Or should I?" Emma turned to me, her blue eyes bright like she was just as excited as I was to try this thing out.

"You go first," I said. "Show off those backflips you used to do on your trampoline back in the day."

She laughed. "Yeah, I don't think I'll be attempting that quite yet."

A teenage guy went next, swinging high and then landing on his back several feet ahead of where the girl had landed before him.

More kids followed and the line inched forward. After another few minutes, Emma and I made it to the front.

Emma grabbed hold of the trapeze, the muscles in her arms flexing as she put her weight on them. She and Arie had a vigorous workout regimen to go along with their athletic clothing line. Seeing how amazingly in shape she was after two kids had always made me wish I was more motivated to exercise.

Sure, I was naturally on the thin side—thanks to my mom's genetics—but I envied people who pushed their bodies to be better every day.

Emma gracefully landed in the foam pit and looked back at me with a smile of exhilaration on her face as she moved along the top of the foam cubes to exit the pit.

Once she had climbed out, she stood with her hands on her slender waist and yelled, "Let's see what you've got, Maya!"

"Okay," I said, suddenly not so sure of myself. But I took a deep breath anyway, stood on my tiptoes so I could reach the trapeze without the stool, and with only a few seconds of hesitation, I let myself swing as far as I could over the foam cubes.

My heartbeat skyrocketed as I flew through the air. And then, just when the swing was on its backward dip, I released my grip and dropped, my landing soft as green and black cubes enveloped me.

It wasn't exactly how I imagined landing on a cloud would be, but it was definitely the softest landing I'd ever had.

I probably would have laid there forever, but since I knew there was a whole line of kids waiting for their turn, I sat up, pushed my legs down into the foam cubes beneath me, and started my walk toward the edge of the pit where Emma was waiting for me.

Or, at least, I *tried* to walk toward the edge. Because when I stepped down on the cubes to exit the pit with ease like Emma and all the kids before her had done, my feet just sunk farther down, not having the resistance beneath them like I'd expected.

I took another step, but just like before, it made me sink even farther down so the foam cubes were now at my chest.

What the heck?

My heart raced as I tried to find some sort of purchase for my feet. But the more I pushed down on the cubes to have something under me to walk on, the more I sunk.

How deep was this thing exactly?

I tried to lift my legs for another step, but it felt like they each weighed a hundred pounds.

I looked at the landing behind me to the line of kids waiting for me to exit the pit and found annoyed expressions on a pack of twelve-year-old boys.

Annoyed at the old lady who couldn't get her butt out of their way.

I turned my gaze back to the edge of the pit where Emma was waiting, and though it was only about ten feet away, it felt like miles from how little I was progressing toward it.

How the heck had everyone made this look so easy? Because I was sweating like a very humiliated pig from the exertion, panic flooding over me.

"What am I doing wrong?" I yelled to Emma, my heart racing faster as I felt like I was just sinking farther and farther down with every step I took. "I can barely move."

"I don't know." She shook her head, seeming confused. "I just kind of swam out."

Just swam out?

She *had* been more on top of the foam cubes.

Had sticking my feet down and trying to walk out been the wrong way to go about this?

I continued to fight my way through the foam cubes that were now feeling more like quicksand beneath my feet than anything solid. But the more I tried, the more stuck I felt.

"Are you okay?" Emma asked, concern etched in her eyes. "Do you need me to get help?"

"Maybe." I sighed, feeling the edges of a panic attack starting to come on as I was exhausting myself but getting nowhere. "I'm stuck."

I looked around to see if there was an employee somewhere close with some sort of rescue device. But the only other adults in the vicinity were a middle-aged couple sitting on the bench behind Emma, watching me like I was a beached whale.

How was this happening to me?

Sure I couldn't remember the last time I'd lifted weights, but I couldn't be this far gone, could I?

My face and neck burned hotter, so I took a deep breath and hoped it would help me hold my panic attack at bay.

I can do this.

Just one step at a time.

I'm not going to drown in a stupid foam pit!

But as I continued to exert myself, with very

little progress, I started to feel hopeless that I'd never get out of here.

What a way to die—the day before my twenty-eighth birthday.

The night before I was set to see my all-time favorite rock star in concert.

Ever since I discovered Incognito—the masked singer whose true identity no one knew—I had dreamed of going to one of his concerts. But anytime he had one remotely close to my small town in Southern Utah, the tickets had sold out within minutes and I'd missed out because I couldn't get through the servers fast enough.

But my amazing friend Emma had managed to pull some strings and got us front-row seats to the last concert of his summer tour in Las Vegas tomorrow night. In just over twenty-four hours, I would be singing along to that raspy baritone voice that literally took my breath away every time he belted out the chorus of his new song "Miles Away Next to You."

At least, I would be doing that if I survived this foam pit of doom.

I looked up at Emma, deciding that desperate times called for desperate measures.

"Can you go get Arie? I don't think I'm getting out of here on my own."

When Arie first moved to Maplebridge during Emma and my senior year of high school, his undercover bodyguard's muscles had been front and center in several of my dreams. This was before I realized he was perfect for my best friend and not me.

So if anyone in this trampoline place could save me from this predicament, it would be him.

"I'll get him," Emma said, and then turned to retrieve her husband from the kids' area.

While Emma went to get my rescuer, I continued my slow walk through what felt like quicksand. Amazingly enough, after another thirty seconds, I made it to the side. But when I tried to lift myself out, my arm muscles were shaking so hard I barely budged an inch.

I looked to where Emma had disappeared to and saw her talking to Arie. Her tall, dark-haired husband glanced my way, and in the next second, he was in motion.

Thank goodness. I sighed, some of the tension leaving my body. This nightmare was almost over.

And that was when a deep voice sounded from above. "Maya? Is that you?"

I closed my eyes tight, hoping it was just my overactive imagination that had conjured up the voice that I'd been doing my best to not think about for the past two months.

But when I opened my eyes and tilted my head up to my left, I found myself staring into the eyes of none other than Landon Holloway—the guy I'd grown up next door to.

Also the guy who I hadn't seen since the day I'd rebound made-out with him after calling off my wedding two months ago.

This night was just getting better and better.

CHAPTER TWO

"H-HI LANDON." I forced a smile on my lips and hoped I wasn't as sweaty and red in the face as I felt.

Was it too much to hope that he'd only just walked into the facility and hadn't seen me struggling for the past few minutes? Because I really didn't need another humiliating experience cemented into his mind.

"Hey..." His dark eyebrows knitted together, concern etched in the features of his way-too-handsome face. "My sister-in-law said it looked like you might need help getting out of there. Do you need a hand?"

My whole body flamed hotter as even more embarrassment flooded me.

He might not have been watching me, but I'd

apparently made enough of a scene that he'd been enlisted to save me.

Maybe I should have just let the foam cubes suck me in when they tried.

Arie was supposed to be coming to my rescue, but when he saw Landon, he stopped his advance, pointed to Landon, and then mouthed to me, *"You okay now?"*

And even though having Landon be the one to save me was about the last thing I wanted, I nodded and gave Arie a thumbs-up to let him off the hook.

I really didn't need for it to look like I needed two strong men to get me out of this wretched pit.

I looked back at Landon whose brown eyes were still on me and sighed. "I guess I could use a hand. This pit apparently wants me to live here."

So he bent over and reached his muscular arms out to me.

I placed both of my hands in his warm and calloused ones, and in a matter of seconds, Landon pulled me out and my feet were on solid ground again.

"Thank you," I said, my whole body going weak with relief at finally being out of the pit of doom.

He let go of me and slipped his hands into the pockets of his shorts. "I'm happy I was here to help."

The couple who had been watching me for the past few minutes on a nearby bench moved from their seats, so I went to sit down, needing a moment to catch my breath.

"Are you here by yourself?" Landon sat next to me, which surprised me since I'd expected him to walk back to wherever his sister-in-law had sent him from.

I mean, we had always been friends, but with the way we'd parted the last time we'd been together, I just assumed he would act awkwardly when we eventually came face to face again.

"I came with Emma and her family," I said, leaning back against the wall, not even trying to pretend like I wasn't completely exhausted.

"Emma Howard?" He gave his head a slight shake. "I mean, I guess it's Emma Blackwell now, huh?"

I nodded. "Yeah, when I called her after work, she said she and Arie were bringing their kids here, so I decided to tag along."

Because I was stupid and thought I was still young enough to come to places like this.

"So I'm guessing those bright orange shorts are not your typical workout wear?" He cocked an eyebrow.

My cheeks flushed, and I looked down at the hideous gym shorts. "They wouldn't let me come in here with jeans."

"I've been there." He leaned back against the wall beside me. "Only, when I had to borrow the shorts they were bright purple."

"You're just saying that to make me feel better, aren't you?"

"It really did happen," he said reassuringly. Then his lips lifted into a slow grin. "But yeah, you looked like you could use a little cheering up."

A kid entered the foam pit ahead of us and exited with ease. "How do they make it look so easy?"

Landon shrugged. "I think the trick is spreading as much of your weight out along the foam cubes as possible so you don't sink, and then kind of swimming out."

Swimming out. That was how Emma had described it, too.

"Well, that would have been good to know before I almost died in there."

Landon chuckled and bumped his shoulder next to mine. "You wouldn't have died."

"I almost had a heart attack," I said.

"Well, it's a good thing I came by when I did then. We couldn't have that happening."

We were both quiet for a beat watching the next kid swing on the trapeze ahead of us, and I wondered what Landon thought about running into each other again.

He still wasn't acting like anything was off between us, which was kind of a miracle since I'd thought for sure that the first time we ran into each other again after I'd basically thrown myself into his all-too-alluring arms would be super awkward.

Maybe he'd somehow forgotten about that night?

Or maybe making out with girls who had just called off their wedding was just a regular everyday thing for Landon.

Growing up, he had always been super easy to flirt with, even if we hadn't ever dated. And with those deep brown eyes that could see into a person's soul and movie-star good looks, I couldn't imagine him having a hard time kissing any girl if he wanted to.

"So, how have you been?" He turned his gaze away from the kids and back to me. "I don't know if I've seen you since..." He rubbed his fingers along his chin like he was trying to remember the last time we'd seen each other exactly.

"I think it was the night before you left for your big road trip," I said.

Or more memorably, the night you found me crying on my parents' front porch and used your magic charm to make me feel better.

Then recognition filled his features. "Yeah." He rubbed the back of his neck, his skin flushing slightly pink. "I guess that was the last time."

So maybe what happened between us wasn't an everyday thing for him after all.

Deciding to just push through the awkwardness, I said, "Anyway, to answer your question, I've been okay. Better than I was that night, at least."

"That's good," he said, his eyes seeming to search mine for a moment as if to decide for himself if I was telling the truth. "I'm glad you're doing better."

I pressed my lips together before smacking them. "And how was your grand tour of the United States?"

"My tour?" He furrowed his brow.

"Yeah, you told me you were going on a big road trip across the country," I said, wondering why he seemed confused. "That's what you did, right? My brother wasn't just mowing your lawn for the past two months because you were too lazy to do it yourself?"

"Oh, yeah," he said. "I just forgot that I told you about it." He shrugged. "It was good. Really long, but good."

"Does that mean you're ready for school to start again?"

Landon was a psychology professor at Maplebridge University where I'd received my bachelor's degree. I'd called it good after getting my degree and opened my own floral shop on main street, but Landon was one of those over-achieving, student-body-president-type people who had not only gone on to get his master's degree but his doctorate's degree to boot.

"I think I need a vacation from my vacation," he said, running a hand through his auburn hair. "And then I'll be ready to start teaching again."

"Not having to wake up and go to work every day for the past two months was too hard on you?" I asked, giving him a smirk.

He chuckled. "Yeah, you know me. Lazy-bones Landon."

I laughed with him because Landon Holloway was the least lazy person I knew. He always had something keeping him busy one way or another. In fact, I wouldn't be surprised if he had actually been secretly working out of state the past two months just for the fun of it—using the road trip as an alibi.

The man didn't sit around.

As if to prove right my thoughts about him never sitting still for long, he rubbed his hands along the legs of his pants and stood from the bench. "I should probably get back to helping with my nephew's party." He turned back to me, his gaze seeming to take me in one last time.

My body started to warm up as I wondered what he thought of me.

Had he thought about our impulsive kiss at all since it happened?

I mean, my beloved rock star, Incognito, was still the guy I daydreamed about kissing most since he just had to be the hottest man alive under that black-and-gold masquerade mask that he wore. But that didn't mean I hadn't relived the way Landon's lips had felt next to mine once or twice...or a hundred times over the past two months.

As I wondered what Landon saw and thought about when he looked at me, I remembered I was wearing bright orange shorts at the moment and that he'd watched me almost drown in a foam pit a few minutes go.

Man, so much for looking jaw-droppingly

gorgeous the first time I ran into him again, especially since I was a complete wreck on my parent's porch the last time we were together.

"Well, it was good to see you again, Maya," he said, his brown-eyed gaze meeting mine.

I nodded and stood as well, feeling short next to his tall frame. "Thanks for coming to the rescue."

His lazy grin stretched wide across his lips. "It was my pleasure."

CHAPTER THREE

THE REST of the time spent at the trampoline park turned out to be much less eventful than the first fifteen minutes—thankfully. I'd chosen to stick to the regular trampolines to avoid any more disasters like the foam pit of doom had provided me with. And while it took my heart a full hour to finally get back to its regular heart rate, I did manage to impress Piper and Blair with my backflip skills. So I felt at least a little redeemed by the end of our time out.

"Do you want to grab some ice cream before we call it a night?" Emma asked me when we were putting our shoes on after jumping for two full hours.

"Ice cream sounds great." I slipped my foot into my mint-green sneaker. "Should we go to Kiki's?"

Kiki's was the best ice cream and soda shop in town.

"That's perfect."

So we all walked out of the building and into the parking lot where my old Volkswagen Jetta was parked next to Arie's big black truck.

I was just about to climb in my car when I saw Landon, with a skateboard under his arm, waving goodbye to someone in a minivan.

Had he skateboarded here from his house? That was, like, two miles away.

The van passed by where I stood, and Landon must have noticed me because he nodded and said, "Hey."

"Hi," I said, wondering if I should just continue getting in my car or not.

He started walking toward me, so I decided to wait by my trunk.

"Let me guess," I said when he got within earshot. "You got so tired of being in your car for the past two months that you've decided to ride your skateboard everywhere now."

"Maybe." He lifted the skateboard a little, his eyes crinkling at the corners as he smiled. "But I do actually ride this thing on campus all the time."

"Gotta be the cool professor, right?" I asked.

He shrugged. "You know it." There was a teasing glint in his eye. "I mean, psychology professors are automatically pretty cool, aren't they?"

"I guess so," I said.

"You guess?" He furrowed his brow. "Aren't you the one who had a major crush on our psychology teacher in high school? Seems like being a *college* professor would just make me even cooler than that." He winked.

My jaw dropped. "How do you even remember that?"

He lifted a shoulder. "I sat right behind you in that class. It was hard not to notice you drooling over Mr. Lund."

My face burned as I remembered all the dumb things I had done as a high school senior to get my fresh-out-of-college and only five-years-older-than-me teacher to see me as more than just a seventeen-year-old girl.

Yeah, I'd been stupid back then. And now that I was a decade older, I would totally go back in time and smack some sense into the super boy-crazy version of me and tell her to just chill out and wait until she was older to worry about finding future Mr. Right.

Was it sad that at almost twenty-eight I was way

less interested in tying the knot than I'd been at seventeen?

"I didn't have actual drool coming out of my mouth, did I?" I asked Landon, trying to figure out what he must have thought about me back then.

He just laughed and shook his head. "I'm just giving you a hard time. Because if anyone could pull off dating the older guys, it was you. You were always ahead of the rest of us."

"Well, everyone passed me up long ago," I said. "I'm pretty sure almost everyone in our grade is married by now. Everyone but you and me, I guess."

"You and me?" He raised an eyebrow, a flirtatious look on his face.

"I didn't mean you and me getting married, like, to each other," I hurried to say when I realized what it had sounded like. "I meant me and you are still single." I shook my head. "Like, yeah, that would be weird. Can you imagine being married to each other?"

My face flushed even hotter as he just stared at me with a smirk on his face, clearly enjoying watching me get all flustered. So I elbowed him. "You like watching me put my foot in my mouth just a bit too much."

He laughed. "It's kind of my favorite thing."

I shook my head. "I think I'm going to go now. Emma and her family are probably already at Kiki's."

"Oh nice. I was actually about to skateboard over there myself. I haven't had one of their milkshakes in way too long."

"Do you want to just ride over with me?" I offered since it didn't make sense to make him skate over there.

"Yeah, sure." He stood up straighter. "That would be great."

So I popped the trunk of my car open and he slipped his skateboard inside, and then we drove a few blocks over to Kiki's.

———

"YOU GUYS HAVE any more fun things planned before summer ends?" Landon asked a while later.

We were sitting in a booth at Kiki's with Arie and Emma while their girls were pushing all the buttons on the jukebox in the corner.

And even though Landon loved to tease me to no end, it was actually kind of nice not being the third wheel to the happy couple for once.

"Actually," Emma said, stirring her chocolate

shake with her straw. "Maya and I are headed to Vegas tomorrow to go to a concert."

"A concert? That sounds fun," Landon said, glancing at me out of the corner of his eye. "Who are you going to see?"

"Have you heard of Incognito?"

Landon went still for a moment before frowning. "The singer who wears a mask?"

"Yes!" I nodded enthusiastically, happy that he'd heard of the masked rock star I was obsessed with. "Emma got me amazing tickets for my birthday, so we're finally going to see him tomorrow."

"You seem really excited about that," Landon said.

"You have no idea." Emma laughed. "You should have seen her face when I told her I got the tickets months ago."

"You like him that much then?"

"'Like him' would be an understatement," Emma said.

Landon narrowed his eyes at me. "But you know he's probably super ugly, right?"

"Ugly?" My jaw dropped. How dare he talk about Incognito that way? "How could you even say such a thing?"

Landon took a sip of his milkshake and shrugged

nonchalantly. "Why else would he wear a mask all the time?"

"To keep his privacy," I said, my tone telling him it should be obvious. "I mean, have you seen that jawline or those blue eyes? He probably has to wear the mask for his own safety."

Landon laughed and gave me the look he'd always given me when we were kids and I would go on and on about whatever guy I'd had a crush on that week. "To be honest," he said. "I've never really paid that much attention to his eye color or jawline. I'll have to take a better note next time I see a photo of him"

"Make sure that you do," I said. "And then you can apologize for saying he's ugly."

"And Landon can also start kissing Incognito's poster every night before he goes to bed just like you do too, huh Maya?" Emma said, a teasing glint in her blue eyes.

I shot her a dirty look. "That was one time, okay?"

Emma just laughed. "But if the opportunity arose, you'd totally kiss him, wouldn't you?"

I took a sip from my water then said, "If I was so lucky to have a few minutes alone with him, I'd do more than kiss him."

Emma exchanged glances with Arie and it seemed like they had some sort of unspoken conversation between the two of them.

"What?" I asked, wondering what that look meant. "Why are you two looking at me like that?"

"Should I tell her?" Emma asked Arie.

"Tell me what?" I asked, my gaze darting back and forth between my friends.

"Yes," Arie said. "I think you should tell her now so we can all watch her reaction." Then he gave me a huge grin, like he knew whatever secret he and Emma had would somehow be a big deal to me.

My mind raced as it tried to figure out what they could be talking about. Did it have something to do with tomorrow's concert?

But before I could come up with any real ideas, Emma pressed her lips together. There was excitement in her eyes. "So do you remember how I got you front-row seats to the concert tomorrow?"

"Yeah?" I said the word slowly, wondering what she was getting at.

She wasn't going to tell me that she'd made the whole thing up, was she? The tickets were actually real, right?

"Well," Emma said, dragging the word out. "That's not the best part about the concert."

"What could be better than front-row seats?"

"I guess it depends on how you feel about your ticket not only getting you within an arm's reach away from the stage, but also thirty minutes alone with him after the concert."

My heart stopped and tingles raced across my arms as the magnitude of what Emma had just said washed over me.

Thirty minutes alone.

With Incognito.

The rock star I had serenading me each and every day through the speakers at my floral shop and the man who kissed me in my favorite dreams.

I opened my mouth to say something, but nothing came out as I was rendered completely speechless.

Landon nudged my arm with his and said to Emma and Arie, "I think you may have just sent Maya into shock."

Arie chuckled, and Emma's smile just grew bigger as she asked, "Are you going to be okay, Maya?"

In a voice much too loud for the small ice cream shop, I said, "I'm going to meet Incognito?!"

"You are." Emma smiled, pleased with my reaction to her surprise.

"You're not teasing me or anything, right?"

"No teasing at all," Emma said. "I know he doesn't usually have VIP packages for sale because he's so protective of his identity, but I was able to pull a few strings and he agreed to meet with you backstage after the concert."

My mouth hung open at the extent that Emma and Arie had gone to just to make such a special thing happen for me. Sure, they were loaded and whatever something like this had cost was probably just a small drop in the bucket for them, but still. To get me time alone with Incognito when no one else ever had before was no easy feat.

It must have cost a fortune.

"So you're telling me that in just over twenty-four hours from now, I'll be sitting in a room with Incognito?" I asked, the reality of what she had done for me still not fully sinking in. "And talking to him about whatever I want?"

"And don't forget that you'll be kissing him, too." Landon winked at me, apparently taking what I'd been saying earlier about kissing my favorite rock star to heart.

But I didn't care about Landon's teasing right then because I was going to see Incognito up close.

All alone for thirty minutes.

"So I'm guessing it was a good surprise?" Arie asked, arching one of his dark eyebrows.

I leaned back against the booth. "Um, yeah." I sighed. "You guys basically just told me that tomorrow night will be the best night of my entire life."

Happy birthday to me!

And it looked like my first birthday present to myself tomorrow would be a brand new outfit worthy of being in Incognito's presence.

CHAPTER FOUR

"SO I KNOW you said earlier that things have been good since we last saw each other," Landon said when we were back in my car and driving toward his neighborhood after finishing our shakes. "But I know you were worried about all the things you'd have to do after calling off the wedding. How did it go?"

He wanted to talk about *that*?

Why would he want to talk about that when we could talk about my upcoming evening with Incognito instead? Which was way more exciting than my cancelled wedding.

I tightened my grip on the steering wheel as I remembered those first couple of weeks after ending my engagement. At least I hadn't called off the wedding on the day of, but with only weeks to go before the big day, I still had a lot of things to cancel and a lot of people to apologize to.

I also had a lot of non-refundable deposits to reimburse my parents for because I didn't feel it was fair to stick them with the bills when the wedding wasn't even happening anymore.

Landon must have sensed my hesitancy because when I didn't respond, he said, "You don't have to talk about it if you don't want. After hearing about your plans to kiss Incognito, I just assumed that you didn't get back with Gavin, which made me wonder how everything went after I left."

"You really want me to kiss Incognito, don't you?" I shot him a sideways glance, happy to talk about Incognito instead of the most recent of my long line of failed relationships.

"I'm just a supportive friend," Landon said. "And if you want to kiss your favorite singer, I'm going to encourage you in that goal."

I would have thought nothing else of what he was saying if he wasn't wearing the kind of smile that made me wonder if there was something more behind his words than just being a good friend.

"How very supportive of you," I said. Then I

sighed and decided to answer the rest of his question. "And yes, you are right to assume that Gavin and I are still definitely broken up."

Gavin had been crushed when I told him I couldn't marry him. We'd been engaged for five months and dated for six months before that, so my seemingly sudden change of heart was sure to have shocked him.

But I couldn't marry someone I wasn't fully in love with. It wouldn't have been fair to either one of us.

After the initial hurt, he'd seemed to bounce back quickly enough. He even changed his relation-ship status from "single" to "in a relationship" on social media a couple of weeks ago, so I was sure he was doing just fine now that two months had passed.

Which had been a relief. He deserved to be happy even if we weren't meant to be.

"So you don't regret what you did that night?" Landon asked, a cautious look on his face.

"It needed to happen," I said. "I just wish I'd done it before we'd sent out the wedding invitations."

That part of it had definitely sucked. Having to send out several hundred "never mind, Maya backed out" messages had been humiliating.

I shrugged. "But it's all over with now, so I can hopefully never do anything like that again."

"Are you dating anyone now?" Landon shifted in his seat, his long legs looking like they could use several more inches of space in my small car. "I'm sure you had tons of guys excited over the prospect of taking you out."

"Actually, I've been taking some time to work on myself a bit." I glanced away from the road to look at him. "Obviously, I have had a bit of a problem with rebounding in the past."

"Well." A flirtatious smile lifted Landon's lips at my remark. "I can't really say I minded this particular tendency of yours that night."

And when his gaze fell on my lips for a second, my skin flushed with heat and an image of us kissing on my parents' front porch popped into my mind.

It really had been a good kiss.

For being friends and nothing but friends for the past twenty-three years, Landon and I had certainly been able to turn up the fireworks when the occasion arose.

I pressed my lips together, as if it would bring back the sensation of his lips moving with mine again. Then realizing what I was doing, I shook my head and said, "I still can't believe I did that."

"Things happen." He shrugged. "At least we made our second kiss better than our first."

"Our second kiss?" I frowned, confused. I'd never kissed Landon before that, had I?

"You can't tell me that you forgot." Disbelief covered his voice.

"Was it during spin-the-bottle at one of those parties in middle school?" I furrowed my brow. "Because I kissed a lot of guys playing that game."

He shook his head and put a hand to his chest. "I can't believe you forgot about our wedding."

"*Our* wedding?"

"Yes," he said, like I really should remember such a thing. "Back when your mom babysat me, you and I totally got married. And then after Theo McDonnell pronounced us husband and wife under the apple tree, we kissed."

"Ah, I can't believe I forgot!" I said, remembering the incident.

My mom had a childcare at her house and Landon was one of the kids that she cared for after we walked home from kindergarten together. We'd totally had our own little five-year-old romance going. Whenever his mom came to pick him up after work, he'd always yell, "Bye, honey" to me and I'd yell back, "I'm not your honey" as he trotted down the sidewalk.

Then of course I would always run to him before he got to the front of his house so I could get one last hug, since I never meant what I'd yelled and my five-year-old self secretly wanted to be his honey and marry him someday.

Landon nodded. "Anyway, I'm sure that kiss didn't cause as many fireworks as the kiss you're going to have with Incognito tomorrow night, but you have to admit that it was at least better than the one in your backyard."

"Well, since I still remember our second kiss, I'd say you are probably right on that account," I said. "Though, from as many times as you've brought up me kissing Incognito, I almost get the feeling that you want me to kiss him even more than I do."

That strange look was back on his face again, but he laughed and said, "I'm just teasing you." He rubbed at a spot on his shorts. "But sure, I guess I've always wondered how my abilities compare to that of the rich and famous. I mean, who better to tell me than someone who has experienced both?" He raised his eyebrows, almost like he was daring me.

"Well, I hate to burst your bubble, but even

though it's totally on my bucket list, I can almost guarantee that me kissing Incognito is next to impossible," I said. "Not only does he probably have a handful of bodyguards around him at all times to make sure no one touches him or tries to remove his mask, but I really doubt he's into kissing random fans he's barely met just because they paid for VIP tickets."

"But you're not just some random fan," Landon said. "You're Maya Brown—the girl who, as far as I've ever seen, can get any guy she wants to bow down at her feet."

I laughed. "Now I know you're not being serious."

Landon shrugged, the fabric of his charcoal-colored shirt stretching across his broad shoulders. "I've watched you date dozens of guys through the years, Maya. I'm not just making that up to feed your ego."

"Well, I guess I know who to call when I need a pick-me-up."

"That you do." Landon leaned his head against the head rest and turned his face to the side to look at me lazily. "Though I think we're going to have to agree to disagree on the fact that I still think Incognito has to be super ugly under that mask."

"And I'm telling you that it's impossible." I rolled my eyes. And since I couldn't let Landon leave this car without defending the rock-god that was Incognito to the end, I added, "With a voice and accent like that, he can't be anything but hot."

"It's always the accent that gets you girls, isn't it?" Landon nodded his head slowly. "Always bumps up a guy's hotness level by at least ten percent, huh?"

I laughed because in this, at least, Landon was totally right. "It really does."

Incognito's accent was unnoticeable when he sang, but when he spoke on stage or in the few interviews he did, his Australian accent was hot enough to bring a girl to her knees.

It was definitely a major weakness of mine, anyway.

Landon shook his head and tsked. "I knew I should have gone to Cambridge and majored in 'British accent' when I had the chance."

"I guess you should have," I said.

Though honestly, Landon was the kind of guy who didn't need an accent to attract anyone. He just had to smile at a girl and she'd be his.

Which had always made me wonder why he didn't date more. He certainly had all the qualities most girls I knew were looking for in a guy.

He was smart, tall, funny, ambitious, good-looking. And since I knew from experience, he was also an amazing kisser.

Heck, if we weren't such good friends and I wasn't currently abstaining from my addiction to hot men besides Incognito, I'd probably try to date him myself.

Maybe he just kept himself too busy to keep a serious girlfriend?

He always seemed like he had something to do and somewhere to be even if he only taught a few classes at the university.

I turned onto the road where I'd grown up, drove past my parents' brick home, and turned on my blinker to pull along the curb in front of the ranch-style home with blue siding that Landon had bought from his parents when they moved to St. George to retire.

"Well, thanks for the ride," Landon said, unbuckling his seatbelt and opening the passenger door. "It was fun to hang out with you again. It's been too long."

I nodded and popped open my trunk so he could grab his skateboard. "It was great to see you again, too."

After he retrieved his skateboard and shut the

trunk, he leaned down to speak to me through the rolled down passenger window. "Have a great time at that concert tomorrow. I hope Incognito exceeds all of your expectations."

"I'm sure he will."

And with that, he waved goodbye and walked up to his front door. As I watched him go, I couldn't help but smile about the past couple of hours.

Here, I'd stressed and fretted about running into him again after our last interaction when really, I hadn't needed to worry at all because Landon was the king of chill.

Apparently, even when a girl threw herself in his arms and tried to kiss away her sorrows, he could snap right back and act completely normal after the moment had passed. I could embarrass myself in front of him a million times and he would still have the ability to leave me feeling better about myself by the end of the day.

And even though I sucked at most relationships, I did at least know that when you found a friendship like that, you didn't mess it up.

You pushed all your romantic notions toward your favorite rock star instead, so there would be absolutely no possibility of self-sabotage since there was no chance of anything more than getting your favorite T-shirt autographed.

Yep, I'd save all my romantic imaginings for Incognito. Landon and I would stay safely in the friend zone where we'd always been, because then he'd always be in my life.

CHAPTER FIVE

"THAT WAS...AMAZING!" I said to Emma with a sigh as Incognito left the stage after singing his encore.

We were sitting on padded crimson seats in The Colosseum at Caesars Palace and had just experienced the concert of a lifetime. I had been to several concerts in my life, but until tonight I had never experienced the phenomenon that was Incognito live.

I'd worried his voice may not be as good in real life as it was in his studio recordings, since that happened at most concerts I'd attended, but somehow, that raspy baritone voice had been even better in person. He had literally taken my breath away more times than I could count with his amazing vocals, and his presence on the stage was enigmatic.

He didn't just stand on the stage in front of the crowd. He commanded it, and everyone in the audience had been transfixed to the magnetic man from the first note until the last.

I had told Landon last night that Incognito was a rock god among men, but after tonight, I couldn't help but wonder if that could actually be true.

"Were you watching him while he sang 'Miles Away Next to You'?" Emma asked from beside me, the look on her face telling me she had been as in awe of the performance tonight as I was. "Because for a couple of minutes there, it almost seemed like he was looking right at you. Like the song had been written for you."

"You saw that?" I asked, unable to keep the excitement from my voice at the thought that it hadn't all been in my head. "I thought I'd just been imagining it because I love that song so much."

Emma shook her head, her blue eyes telling me she wasn't joking. "No, it really happened. He was just staring at you the whole time. As if you were the girl he was singing about."

"Do you think he found out ahead of time what seat I was sitting in?" I asked, feeling breathless as I remembered how it felt to have his blue eyes on me as he sat on a stool with an acoustic guitar, singing a stripped-down version of his famous love ballad. "That way he could give me special attention during the concert because of the VIP package?"

"I have no idea. But either way, I'm pretty sure every single girl in the audience tonight wanted to be you." Emma shook her head. "Heck, I'm happily married to Arie, but for a minute there I was totally spellbound by him."

"It was crazy!" I nodded my agreement. "And I'm pretty sure I figured out why he wears the mask."

"Why?"

"Because us mere humans wouldn't be able to handle the allure that Incognito has. Like how the bible says something about how man couldn't handle facing God because of how amazing he is. I think Incognito is like that."

Emma laughed at my comparison. "Like Incognito is a literal Rock God?"

I laughed, knowing it sounded ridiculous. But since it totally seemed like it could be true, I said, "Exactly."

"Well, I guess if anyone could hold that title, it would be him," Emma said.

"Totally." I sighed dreamily.

Then my eyes caught on the clock on the wall. I broke out of my trance as I realized I only had twenty minutes until I was slotted to meet with Incognito backstage.

"Crap!" I said, gathering my purse that had my phone and the new Incognito T-shirt I'd bought before the concert for him to sign. "I need to find the VIP waiting area or I'm going to miss this once-in-a-lifetime chance."

AFTER WALKING me to the VIP waiting area, Emma said goodbye and headed back to our hotel room in Caesars Palace.

Usually at concerts, there was a long line of people with VIP tickets waiting for their turn to meet the star, but when I got there, there were only a couple of men and a woman all wearing black with security badges.

Did these security people know his true identity?

Or were they, like me, just as curious about who he was beneath the mask?

You could only keep your identity a secret for so long if you were letting people in on the secret. He probably had to be super careful who he let into his circle of trust, because if that circle got too big it would only be a matter of time before someone who knew him in real life figured out who he was and spilled the beans to the world.

Though, since he was from Australia and touring in the US, it was probably safer here than if he was in his own hometown and had more of a chance of running into someone he knew.

A woman in a black skirt suit and security badge came from the door that led to the backstage area.

"Maya?" she asked, looking at me expectantly.

"Yeah, that's me." I swallowed and nodded, butterflies taking flight in my stomach over the thought that my time slot had come.

"Great." She smiled, making some sort of note on the clipboard in her hand. "It'll be about five more minutes, okay?"

"Okay," I said, relaxing just a little and taking a deep breath.

Then she turned back to where she'd come from and I was back to waiting anxiously for my time.

Last night after getting back to my apartment, I had been so amped up over the prospect of having this time alone with Incognito that I'd made up a whole list of questions that I could ask him if my nerves happened to take over.

I wasn't normally an anxious person by nature and had never had trouble holding up my end of a conversation, but I'd also never been face to masked face with my favorite singer either, so I wanted to make sure I had planned for anything.

So as I waited, I pulled out my phone from my purse to look over the questions and make sure there wasn't anything I'd missed. But when I checked, the home screen showed that I had missed a text from Landon.

I swiped my thumb across the message to read it.

Landon: **I forgot to wish you Happy Birthday earlier, so Happy Birthday!! I hope it's as awesome as you are.**

Well, that was sweet of him to remember.

The message had been sent only five minutes ago, so it was likely he was still awake. I decided to respond.

Maya: **Thanks for remembering! Since I was just reminded that you are my first husband, I have to applaud you for not falling for the stereotype by actually remembering your wife's birthday. ;)**

Landon: **I could never forget my first love, even if she broke up with me halfway**

**through kindergarten when Taylor Velario
moved in.**

I smiled at the memory. Taylor Velario had been
pretty cute back then, with spiky blond hair and the
cutest dimples.

Landon: **My childhood heartbreak aside,
I hope the concert with Incognito was
everything you hoped it would be.**

Maya: **The concert was AMAZING. And
btw, there's no way that man is ugly
beneath the mask.**

Landon: **I guess we'll never know until
he decides to show us. Just remember the
plan and make sure to kiss him tonight so
you can tell me how I compare. ;)**

I chuckled. Either Landon thought I was much
bolder than I really was and would kiss near-
strangers, or he assumed that Incognito was the type
of rock star who kissed every girl he met with.

But since we were just having fun, I said: **If
he asks me to kiss him, then I will
oblige.**

I mean, who wouldn't?

Landon: **Promise?**

I shook my head and smiled. I'd never had a guy

rooting for me to kiss another man so much in my life.

Since I knew there was a zero percent chance of a kiss with Incognito being on the table, I texted back: **I promise.**

The security lady who had come out a few minutes ago came back through the door. "Incognito is ready to see you now."

CHAPTER SIX

I FOLLOWED the lady in black down a dimly lit hall past several doors until we came to a door with a star-shaped placard that read: Incognito.

My hands went tingly and anticipation flooded my system.

Behind that door was the most amazing singer in the whole world. And in just a few seconds, I would be one of the few people to ever have significant time alone with him.

This was unreal.

I pinched myself, not truly believing this was actually happening.

"He should be right inside," the security lady said, and instead of leading me inside to introduce me like I expected, she simply opened the door a crack and gestured for me to walk in.

I swallowed and straightened my shoulders, and after taking one more deep breath, I creaked the door farther open and stepped inside.

The room was pretty dark when I walked in, the overhead lights turned down with just a few lamps lighting the corners. I didn't know what exactly I had expected when I walked into the room, but for some reason I had expected it to look different than this. Brighter, at least.

But I supposed the dim lighting was probably just an extra precaution to make sure that even up close, Incognito's identity was safe.

There was a small couch straight across from me. Photos of artists who had previously had residencies at The Colosseum hung on the walls. One side had a few dressing tables with backlit mirrors for the hair and makeup team to work their magic on the performers before the show.

There were other tables and chairs scattered around the room. A cheese board with various meats, cheeses, veggies, fruits, and crackers sat on the coffee table. And another tray with what looked like a Very Cherry Ghirardelli Chocolate Cheesecake, which just so happened to be my favorite dessert, was set next to the cheese board.

Was I going to be eating these delicious foods with Incognito tonight? Because my stomach rumbled at the sight of so much good food.

Speaking of Incognito, where was he?

"Hello?" I called out, wondering if he might be behind the curtain at the back of the room, which served as a makeshift wall.

At my greeting, the curtain pulled open to reveal a tall man with broad shoulders, brown hair, the most amazing jawline, and the signature black-and-gold masquerade mask.

Incognito.

Oh my goodness!

He slipped his phone into his back pocket, like he'd just been using it, a hint of a smile on his lips, and then he looked at me.

"Sorry, I was just putting my mask back on after my shower," he said, his Australian-accented voice filling the quiet room. "You must be Maya."

He stepped forward until we were only a couple feet apart and held his hand out for me to shake.

"H-hi," I said, placing my trembling hand in his, suddenly overwhelmed with his presence. "I-I can't believe this is really happening."

He covered our hands with his other hand in a comforting gesture, like he understood exactly how nervous and excited I was to be meeting him but wanted me to feel comfortable in his presence. "Would you like to take a seat? It looks like my team has refreshments set up for us."

I nodded, unable to speak because the hands that had just played riff after riff on his Gibson SG were currently touching my skin. And it felt amazing, sending little sparks of electricity all the way up my arm.

He seemed to realize just how in awe of him I was because his grin stretched wider and he gently pulled me toward the brown leather couch.

Thankfully, even though my mind was going haywire, my legs were at least able to follow his lead and I took a seat on the cushion to the right.

I expected Incognito to take one of the chairs opposite the couch since I was a stranger to him, but he surprised me by sitting on the cushion on the other end of the couch, close enough that I caught a faint whiff of his shampoo or body wash.

Holy crap, he smelled so good.

I'd seen a few interviews on YouTube where the interviewer had commented on how good he smelled, and yeah, they weren't exaggerating.

I drew in another breath as he got comfortable but told myself that was the last one, because I did not need to hyperventilate during this meeting just because I was trying to inhale him.

"So did you enjoy the concert?" He turned to me, his blue eyes showing through the eye slots of his mask. "I think I remember seeing you on the front row with a friend."

He remembered seeing me? I squealed a little on the inside.

"Yes, I came with my best friend, Emma," I said. "And you were amazing tonight."

"Yeah?"

I nodded. "I know you probably hear this all the time, but tonight was probably the best concert I've ever been to. You were a master on that stage."

His full pink lips stretched into a smile at my compliment. "I'm glad you enjoyed it."

"Oh, I did. I'm pretty sure tonight just might be the best birthday I'll ever have."

By a long shot.

Man, talk about peaking before I was even thirty.

He just laughed at my over-enthusiasm. "So is today your actual birthday?"

I nodded. "Yes."

"Then happy birthday," he said. "And how old are you?"

"Twenty-eight," I said. "I'm just six months younger than you."

He was quiet for a beat too long, and that was when I realized how that sounded.

I covered my mouth with my hands before saying, "Sorry, that makes me sound like a total stalker."

He laughed and seemed to relax a little. "It's okay. I sometimes forget that people actually care about those details about me."

"Why wouldn't they?" I asked, confused at why he'd be surprised. I was pretty sure most of the famous celebrities like him had all kinds of personal details like that posted on their IMDb or Wikipedia pages.

But he just shrugged and said, "I guess since I live a pretty regular life most of the time it's easy to pretend like Incognito—" He pointed to the mask. "—is another person, in a way. I mean, for the most part I just feel like a regular human who sometimes gets to do a really cool job."

A regular human?

Of course he'd say that. To have the level of

talent that he had yet choose to avoid the notoriety he could have in his everyday life by keeping his true identity a secret just went to show how humble this guy was.

"Anyway." He smoothed his hands along the thighs of his dark jeans. "Since it's your birthday, and we do have this delicious cheesecake, how about we call it your birthday cake and dig in?"

"That sounds amazing to me," I said. "I mean, it's probably just a coincidence, but that flavor of cheese-cake is actually my favorite."

"It is?" he asked, picking up a long knife from the table and cutting into the cake. "That is an awesome coincidence."

But even though he acted surprised, it almost looked like he was fighting back a smile as he cut two large wedges of the cake and set them on gold paper plates.

Had Emma told his manager this was my favorite birthday dessert when she arranged this?

She *was* full of surprises, so that would make sense.

"This one is for the birthday girl." He handed me one of the plates. Then taking his own plate in his hands, he leaned back into the cushions.

I took a bite of the cake, just to see if it was as good as I remembered. As the cherry and chocolate flavors hit my taste buds, it took all of my self-control not to moan over how delicious it was.

"From the look on your face right now, I'm guessing it tastes okay?" Incognito asked, a slight smile on his lips as he watched me basically having a spiritual experience.

"It's perfect." I was pretty sure it tasted even better than the other times I'd tried this exact recipe.

"Good," he said then took a bite of his own piece.

I watched him to see if he liked it, and when his eyes lit up as he savored the taste, I smiled and said, "You're a fan, too?"

"Definitely a fan." He smiled and dug his fork in for a second bite.

I was bonding over cheesecake with Incognito!

Yes, I was probably going to fangirl over every little thing we did during this once-in-a-lifetime, thirty-minute meeting because every second spent with Incognito was like a dream come true. And I needed to remember every single detail so I could relive this night over and over again.

After chewing and swallowing his second bite of cake, Incognito wiped his mouth with a napkin then turned back to me. "So, now that I know you have good taste in desserts, I'd love to get to know a little more about you, Maya. Where are you from? Las Vegas?"

This über famous rock star wanted to find out more about a regular girl like me?

I cleared my throat, suddenly nervous to talk about myself. "I'm actually from a small town in Southern Utah called Maplebridge. It's just a couple of hours from here."

"Born and raised there?" he asked.

"Basically," I said. "My family moved there when I was five and I never left."

"Must be a great place."

"It is," I said. "Though I'm sure anywhere you call home is special. Like how you probably miss Australia while you're on tour."

He frowned as if confused, but after a moment he seemed to realize something and said, "Ah, yes. Good old Australia."

Well, that was kind of a weird reaction.

Why did he say it like that?

"Do you not miss Australia then?" I slid my fork into my cheesecake to serve myself another bite.

I guess not everyone loves the place they grew up in.

He lifted a shoulder in a shrug. "It's hard to miss a place when you've never been there."

Wait.

I froze.

What did he just say?

I blinked my eyes a few times as I ran his last sentence through my mind again. As realization hit me, I gasped and said, "You're not from Australia?"

His smile stretched across his lips, showing a row of perfectly white teeth, before he held up his hand holding the fork and said, "In my defense, I've never once claimed to be from Australia. So I never actually lied about it."

I pulled my head back. "But you have an Australian accent."

"Sure." He nodded, acknowledging that fact at least.

"Are your parents from Australia and so you picked up the accent from them?" I asked. "Or is the accent fake?"

"Does it sound fake?" A dark eyebrow peeked up over the top of his mask.

"Well, no..."

But that didn't mean it wasn't. Actors used fake accents all the time on TV. It wouldn't be too hard for him to have simply created the Australian accent as a way to keep people from figuring out his true identity.

"So your friend said you're my biggest fan," he said, changing the subject and not really giving me a straight answer about the origin of his accent. "And since I don't meet with fans very often and try to avoid the Internet like the plague, I'm always curious what you all believe about me."

"Well, I'm sure it goes without saying, but until about a minute ago I believed you were from Australia."

A smirk played on his lips. "Which now you likely feel betrayed over the fact that I'm not."

"So betrayed," I said, but I gave him a flirtatious smile so he'd know I wasn't too mad.

"And are you going to leave this meeting with me to tell all the world that I'm not actually from Australia?" he asked.

I sensed a wariness in his eyes. Like he was worried he'd made a mistake in trusting me with this information. So I quickly shook my head. "I'd never do that to you."

"Promise?" That dark eyebrow of his was peeking over his mask again.

"Of course."

"Well, good." A smile was back on his lips.

"Because now that one cat is out of the bag, I thought it might be fun to play a little game with you."

"A game?"

He nodded. "I've always been fascinated in the way people think about certain things, and so even though I love my privacy, sometimes I also think it would be nice to dispel some of the rumors that go around about me."

"You would?"

"Yes," he said. "And you seem like a trustworthy-enough fan that I could maybe let you in on a few secrets and trust them to be kept safe."

"Really? You trust me that much?" My chest fluttered at the thought that this guy whom I had idolized for the past three years could already put that much faith in me.

Maybe he'd done some sort of background check on me before agreeing to meet?

"I'm really good at reading people, and even though we've just met I can tell that you're a loyal friend," he said.

So far his estimation of me was correct. I'd always kept my friends' secrets. Even the big, crazy ones like how Arie was originally Emma's under-cover bodyguard—a secret they'd wanted to keep on the down low for years until they felt safe enough for everyone else to know.

So I could most definitely be trusted with whatever Incognito wanted me to know about him.

He set his half-eaten cake on the coffee table, so I did the same.

"Anyway." He grabbed a pitcher of water and filled the two glasses that sat on the table. "Since I can't have you going out into the world and telling everyone that I'm a boring old hack, we'll turn this little 'getting to know the real you' session into a game."

"That involves water?" I scrunched up my nose, hoping we weren't going to be pouring water on each other. I mean, I didn't just buy my new outfit today to have it ruined.

"Don't all fun games in the summer involve water?" he asked, the corner of his lip quirking up.

"My younger brothers would certainly agree with that." Growing up, they and Landon had definitely had too much fun turning most of my suntanning sessions into water fights.

"Brothers are usually fun like that." He laughed. Then after setting the pitcher back on the table, he handed me a glass of water and took his own. "So this is the game. We're going to test your discerning skills here."

"My discerning skills?"

He nodded. "Yes. I'm sure there are all sorts of wild stories about me on the Internet, so this is your chance to debunk them. For every fact you guess right, I will have to take a sip of water. But for every fact you get wrong, you have to take a sip of water."

"So like the Never Have I Ever game but without the alcohol?"

"I guess." He shrugged. "We're kind of limited on our party game resources back here so it's the best idea I have."

"I think it sounds fun," I said, not wanting him to think I was above playing his spur-of-the-moment game idea when just being in his presence was exhilarating.

"So are you in?" he asked.

"Of course. As long as you think it's fair." Because I was pretty much obsessed with the man and had watched every interview he had ever done.

"Like I said, I'm interested in finding out what you really believe about me." There was a challenge in his dark blue eyes that showed a confidence I never would've had if I were in his position.

But since he was the one making up the game

and deemed it fair, I lifted my glass in the air and said, "I hope you're prepared to get a really full bladder because—not to sound creepy or anything—I probably have your Wikipedia page memorized."

He laughed and clinked his glass against mine. "Then this should be interesting."

CHAPTER SEVEN

I PRESSED my lips together and studied his face as I tried to figure out what to ask him—or at least, what I could see of his face with the mask covering most of it.

What fact did I want to verify about Incognito first?

It was hard to decide. There were several things that I thought I'd known for sure about him before we met—like how he was from Australia—but since that was clearly not true, I was starting to second guess everything.

Was that even his real hair color?

Were those muscles real?

Were his deep ocean-blue eyes really his natural color?

Or had all those things been distorted with hair dye, pec implants, or colored contacts?

I really didn't know.

"Did you forget that Wikipedia page you memorized?" he asked, his eyes locking with mine, making me feel warm with how he was studying me.

But I feigned the confidence I'd had before and said, "No."

"Trying to decide if it's safe to ask me about the secret families I have hidden in each city I visit?" he asked, amusement in his eyes.

"I haven't heard that one, actually," I said.

"Well." He smiled. "It's a good one."

"I'm sure certain fans would eat that up," I said, holding my glass of water close to my chest with both hands. "But, like I said, I'm one of those good fans who knows you're not like that. So I guess I'll go with the rumor that the reason why you keep your identity a secret is because you're actually a prince of some small country off the coast of Australia and your father doesn't approve of your music."

"You think I'm a prince?"

I shrugged. "I'm just testing the most exciting theories right now."

"Well, I did already tell you that I'm just a

regular human, so sadly, I'm not secretly a prince. So drink up."

"I guess I should have known." I swallowed a sip of water. "You did say the accent was fake."

"I don't think I ever actually did, though." He winked.

"Fine then. Here's my next assumption: your Australian accent is fake and you created it to throw fans off from knowing you're really from the United States."

He bit his lip, not moving as anticipation grew over me at finding out this secret. Then finally, he shook his head and took a sip of water.

"I knew it!" I bounced in my seat, a little water splashing out the top of my glass onto my jeans.

"But you're not going to tell anyone else that, right?" He raised an eyebrow.

I made the zipping-my-lips gesture and said, "Your secret is safe with me."

"Okay, give me your next guess." He lifted one of his long legs onto the couch, like he was settling in.

I thought about it for a moment before saying, "You've been approached by several A-list stars to donate DNA to give them the perfect specimen of a baby."

His eyes went wide as if I'd just shocked him with that rumor.

"Surprised people know about it?" I asked.

He shook his head. "People actually believe that?"

I lifted my shoulders. "Why wouldn't they? Rumor has it that part of the reason why you wear the mask is because us mere humans couldn't handle gazing upon your real face because it's too amazing to look at."

That earned me a huge smile and a shake of the head. "My fans certainly have wild imaginations."

"So it's not true?" I asked.

"That I have been approached by multiple women to donate my DNA?"

"Well, that and the other."

He lifted the glass of water to his mouth and took a sip.

My jaw dropped. "That's actually true? Do you have lots of Incognito babies running around Hollywood Boulevard?"

He rolled his eyes. "As if. Yes, they may have asked. But no, I did not accept the offer. If I have any children of my own, I will be the one to raise them myself." He took a breath, "And as for your other assumption that I am too amazing to look at... Well, how arrogant would I sound if I said it was true?"

"So it is true?"

He shook his head. "Of course not. I'm just a regular guy. I wouldn't say I'm ugly, but I don't, like, cause car accidents everywhere I go because women can't take their eyes off of me."

I laughed. "I guess I get to tell my friend Landon that he was wrong in that at least."

"Your friend Landon?" Incognito cocked his head to the side as if the topic interested him.

"Yeah, he tried to tell me last night that the only reason why you wear the mask is because you're ugly as mud."

"Ugly as mud, huh?" He scratched his chin.

"Maybe not ugly as mud exactly. But just in need of a disguise, I guess." I waved my hand. "I'm sure he was just saying that to rile me up. He's kind of obsessed with teasing me."

"And he's just your friend?" Incognito narrowed his eyes, and for a second the look in them almost reminded me of someone else.

But the whisper of familiarity was gone before I could figure out who he reminded me of. I mean, I'd certainly remember gazing into eyes like his, wouldn't I?

I licked my lips and tried to remember his question. Then I said, "Yeah, Landon and I are just friends."

But even as I said it, the memory of us kissing on my parents' front porch filled my mind and I wondered if two people who were just friends would have kissed like that.

I hadn't exactly kissed any other guy friends like that before.

But I couldn't have feelings for Landon.

That would be crazy.

Especially since I had a major crush on the guy I was currently sitting on a couch with.

Incognito pursed his lips as he studied me, and either he was a psychic or just really good at reading people like he'd said before, but the next words out of his mouth were, "It almost seems like there's more to you and this friend than you're saying."

CHAPTER EIGHT

"WE'RE JUST FRIENDS, REALLY," I said.

"You sure about that?" Incognito asked. "Because from the look on your face, it almost seems like there's something more you aren't telling me."

I didn't know what it was that had me spilling the beans to Incognito when I hadn't even told Emma about that night, but I found myself saying, "We kissed. Once." Then I shook my head. "Well, technically twice, but the first time was when we were five so that doesn't really count."

Incognito's eyes lit up and he leaned forward and said, "Sounds like the oldest story in the book to me."

I frowned, not understanding what he meant.

"Girl and guy are friends," he explained in his deep, fake accented voice. "Girl and guy flirt all the time. Guy gets feelings for the girl because she's amazing. But since he's friend-zoned he can't do anything about it. Then something happens to get them to finally kiss and things get confusing until the girl either tells him it's never happening or she lets him out of the friend zone."

I laughed when he had finished. "Sounds like a story you might know a little too well."

"Eh." He put his arm along the back of the couch and strummed his fingers. "I might have experienced it once or twice."

Someone had put Incognito in the friend zone?

Who would be stupid enough to do something like that?

"And how did it end? Did you get out of the friend zone?"

He pulled on his bottom lip with his teeth, considering his answer for a moment before saying, "It's still to be determined."

"So you're in the confusing stage?" I raised an eyebrow.

"You could say that."

Well, that sucks. I sighed, disappointed that Incognito had another woman in his life. I knew I really shouldn't be surprised since guys like him were never single.

"Why does it suck?" he asked.

I looked up at him again. "What?"

"You said it sucks that I'm still in the confusing stage with this girl."

"I said that out loud?"

He nodded, a mischievous look in his eyes.

I groaned. "Well, just pretend like you didn't hear that."

"But why?"

"Because it's embarrassing.

"Embarrassing, how?"

I sighed again and shook my head. I might as well just say it. It wasn't like I'd ever see him again, so embarrassing myself in front of him couldn't really hurt me that much.

So I went ahead and threw my ego to the side for a moment and said, "Because even though it's probably completely obvious, since I'm your number one fan who memorizes lots of Wikipedia facts about you—"

He held up a finger to correct me. "Lots of incorrect Wikipedia facts."

I rolled my eyes. "Okay, fine. So the Internet has failed me a lot." I breathed. "But I'm sure you probably already guessed that I totally have a crush on you, and so like with all number-one fans, I'm not exactly thrilled about the fact that you're totally in love with someone else."

And when I looked up at him again, he had a huge grin on his masked face.

Either he loved hearing that his fans were in love with him, or he was just really enjoying watching me embarrass myself right now.

Incognito was about to say something when there was a knock on the door. We both turned and saw the woman who had brought me here standing in the doorway.

Was my time already up?

She looked at Incognito who had sat up straighter at her interruption and said, "Just three more minutes."

"Thank you, Miranda," Incognito said, and the woman nodded and ducked out, shutting the door behind her.

When we were alone again, Incognito turned back to look at me. "Any last things you want to clear up before you leave?"

I thought about it, trying to remember all the questions I had planned to ask him before coming here. Sure, I'd learned a few things, but the time had gone way too quickly.

"Would you mind if I got a selfie to remember

meeting you tonight?" I asked. "I promise I won't put it on the Internet if you don't want me to."

"Sure." He stood from the couch, his over six-foot height towered over me. Then he looked around the room for a second before pointing toward one of the corners with a lamp. "That corner looks like it has the best lighting for a photo."

"Perfect."

He offered a hand to help me stand, and when I set mine in his, sparks shot through my arm just like they had before. But this time there was almost something familiar about the way his hand felt in mine. Like I'd touched him for more than just a few seconds before.

But that couldn't be possible. The man behind the mask couldn't be someone I'd spent time with before, could he?

I met his gaze as he helped me up and found an intense look in his eyes—almost like he knew or expected me to feel a strange sense of déjà vu.

But instead of saying anything about it, he cleared his throat and said, "Let's get you that photo."

When he let go of my hand to lead me to the corner, the warmth of the last few seconds went away.

As I followed him, I went over in my mind the last thirty minutes we'd shared. For someone who didn't do many meet-and-greets, Incognito had seemed really at ease around me. He'd even been transparent enough to let me in on a few of the secrets no one else knew about him.

And as we talked, the conversation had been effortless—almost like we were old friends just catching up.

Sure there were people who could talk to strangers like they'd known them their whole life, and maybe his personality was just so outgoing that he could shoot the breeze with anyone.

But was that really something you would expect from someone who kept his life so private? It didn't seem likely.

We made it to the corner and Incognito turned to me. "Do you want me to take the photo since my arms are longer than yours?"

"S-sure," I said. Then I fumbled around in my purse for a moment to pull out my phone.

But when I looked at the lock screen with a photo of Incognito set as the wallpaper, it showed a missed text message from Landon twenty-eight minutes ago.

Landon: **Just don't show Incognito all**

your kissing skills. I hear they have been responsible for distracting guys on road trips for months at a time.

I swiped a shaky thumb across the screen as fast as I could to bring up the photo app, hoping Incognito didn't see Landon's text or the fact that I was such a huge fan that I had his photo greet me every time I picked up my phone.

But I must not have been fast enough because he said in a low voice, "Your friend-zoned friend wants you to kiss me?"

I froze and my phone slipped from my hand, landing on the carpeted floor with a thump.

"Y-you weren't supposed to see that," I hurried to say. I was about to reach down to pick up my phone so I could just bolt from the room with it, but Incognito bent over and swiped it up. But instead of handing it to me, he kept it.

He pressed his lips together as if debating his next words and said, "Would you have let me kiss you if I'd tried?"

What?

I just looked at those big blue eyes of his, the eyes that I had stared at so many times on my phone when I listened to his music.

The eyes that seemed to be looking into my soul as he waited for me to answer.

"You're asking if I'd let you kiss me?" I breathed, my pulse suddenly pounding in my temples.

He stepped closer, and with the hand that wasn't holding my phone, he reached up to tuck some hair behind my ear, his fingers slowly trailing a path of fire along my skin as he moved his hand to cup the back of my neck.

"Yes, Maya Brown. Would you?"

And when his eyes flitted to my lips, my brain went into complete overload.

"I— um—wha—?" I blinked my eyes shut and shook my head, trying to get my mouth to form actual words instead of random syllables.

He must have known exactly what he was doing to me, because his lips quirked up into his signature half-smile and he stepped closer.

"I have to admit..." He bent over so he was whispering the words next to my ear, sending chills racing down my spine. "That I'm more than a little curious what it's like to experience the kind of kiss known to distract a guy for months at a time."

I released a shaky breath, sure I was about to faint. Any moment now my legs were going to collapse beneath me and I would melt into a puddle at Incognito's feet.

When he pulled back so I could see his eyes again through the holes in his mask, there was a vulnerability that hadn't been there a second ago. Like he was nervous and the confident exterior was simply a facade.

That was when I finally found the courage to whisper, "Then maybe you should come closer and find out."

But just as he was tilting my head back in what I was sure was about to be my first kiss with my celebrity crush, the door behind us opened.

No!

In my mind, I urged Incognito to ignore the security guard who was stepping inside the room, so I could find out if kissing the famous rock star was anything like I'd imagined in my daydreams. But he froze the moment he realized we weren't alone anymore, and in the next instant, he dropped his hand and stepped back to put another foot of space between us.

"Sorry to interrupt," the woman he'd called Miranda earlier said. Even though the room was dimly lit, I could tell she was embarrassed for catching us a breath away from each other.

"It's okay," Incognito mumbled. "We were just about to take a photo." And as if to prove that we most certainly had not been about to kiss, he held up my phone. "Would you mind snapping the photo for us since you're here?"

Miranda nodded. "Of course."

She crossed the room and Incognito handed her my phone while I just stood there dumbly, still so caught off guard by this whole situation.

Had Incognito really been about to kiss me?

Like, had it almost happened for real?

I pinched myself to make sure I was still awake, and yep, this was all really happening.

Miranda stepped in front of us so her back was to the lamp, and when she held my phone up, Incognito slipped his muscular arm behind my waist, sending tingles up my side with the unexpected touch.

"Don't forget to smile," he said into my hair as he squeezed me closer to him.

So I looked ahead and gave the camera lens aimed at us my best smile, my cheeks shaking slightly from how overwhelmed I was with all of this.

Miranda snapped a few photos then said, "Is that all?"

"Yes," I said. "Thank you."

She handed the phone back to me, and I slipped

it into my purse that was still hanging in the crook of my arm.

"If you could just wait for us outside the door, Miranda," Incognito said. "I want to take a moment to say goodbye to Maya."

Miranda nodded dutifully, and within a few seconds it was just me and Incognito in the room again.

He took my hand in his, smoothing his thumb along my knuckles.

"I know this is probably crazy of me to ask," he said. "But if I was to come to Maplebridge next weekend, would you let me see you again?"

My eyes widened, caught off guard by his question. "You want to visit me?"

He nodded, his eyes darting back and forth between mine. "I have a few things to take care of this next week, but my tour is over and I'd love to see you again if you let me. I rarely ever have such an instant connection with someone."

"Seriously?" I asked. "Like, you're not just saying this so I don't tell everyone that you're not really from Australia?"

"I'm serious." He smiled. "Plus, we never really finished our game earlier and I'm sure there are a lot of misconceptions I still need to clear up."

"Okay," I said. Then realizing that sounded way less enthusiastic than this epic moment deserved, I hurried to add, "I mean, of course I'd love to see you again."

"Great." He squeezed my hand one more time and then said, "I guess I better walk you to the door. I'm sure Miranda is ready to get to bed and she can't do that until I'm back on my tour bus."

He tugged on my hand, and we walked to the door where once I was out of this room, this magical night would become a memory. A really, really good memory.

"I'll be in touch," he said, and before I knew what was happening, he was pulling me toward him and wrapping his arms around me in a hug.

As he enveloped me against his toned, muscular torso, that sense of déjà vu was back again.

He smelled amazing, and while my mind was racing a hundred miles a minute, I still couldn't get past the feeling that there was something so familiar about his embrace.

But I would know him if I'd seen him before, right?

I'd remember his blue eyes, his strong jaw, the contours of his chest that my head was now resting on. And yet, even though he seemed so familiar to me, I couldn't conjure up a picture of the face hidden behind the mask.

His hands rubbed along my back, like he wanted to savor the moment as much as I did—like he truly had enjoyed the last thirty minutes as much as I had and didn't want to let me go.

This was just crazy.

Sure, it was believable for *me* to get wrapped up in this fairytale since I'd dreamed of something like this happening since I first fell in love with his hypnotic voice and mesmerizing eyes. But for *him* to respond like this was unthinkable.

Then again, his eyes had been on me the whole time he'd sang my favorite song tonight. So maybe it was just one of those kismet things where there was an instantaneous connection that wouldn't be denied.

"Maya..." he mumbled my name next to my ear, his accented voice so low and husky it made my stomach twist up in knots.

"Yeah?" I gazed up at him, and there was a look in his eyes that I didn't expect. He looked almost tortured.

"There's something I should tell you," he whispered. "Before this goes too far."

My eyebrows knitted together as I studied what I could see of his face.

"It's just..." He sighed, running a hand through his hair. "I just don't want you to be disappointed."

Be disappointed?

What was he talking about?

"I could never be disappointed by you," I whispered. He had been nothing but amazing tonight—exceeding all my hopes and dreams of what this meeting would be like.

"But you might," he whispered back.

He sighed again, his eyes darting back and forth between mine like he was trying to decide what to do.

But then his gaze went down to my lips again. And I knew it was probably crazy for me to even consider it, but I allowed my impulsive side to take over—the same impulsive side that had overtaken me the night Landon and I had kissed.

So before Incognito could tell me whatever he thought might disappoint me, I decided to shoot my shot by pushing myself onto my tiptoes and kissing him.

Right on the lips.

Instead of responding in the way I had hoped, he went still. So still that I worried he might pull away and decide he didn't want to kiss me. Like maybe this wasn't the kind of kiss that could distract a guy for months after all.

But he didn't push me away the moment our lips connected. Instead, he made a quiet groaning sound at the back of his throat, and then he was kissing me back.

His lips were moving with mine, and he pulled me closer against him, kissing me like he *wanted* to.

And even though I had been the one to initiate the kiss, it was soon obvious that I wasn't the only one responsible for it anymore. He led my lips in a give and take that instantly left me breathless.

I was kissing Incognito!

How was this even my life?

I didn't understand it at all, but at that moment, I didn't need to figure it out. I just wanted to enjoy this impossible moment and soak in everything that was happening.

So when he took my hips in his hands and walked me backwards until my back was pressed against the wall, I let him. And when he traced his hands up my sides until his fingers were tangled in my hair, I reveled in it. And when he deepened the kiss, I did the same.

I let my hands trace their way along his sides,

feeling the ribbed muscles just beneath the thin fabric of his T-shirt. I let them slip up his torso and higher up to his chest. He obviously had an excellent workout routine, even on tour, because he was trim and toned and felt absolutely amazing.

His lips broke away from mine for a second to trail kisses along my jaw, and I couldn't get over how comfortable we were with each other. Like even though we'd never kissed before—never even been in the same room until tonight—we seemed to be made to kiss each other. The rhythm was so natural and easy. It was like we'd done this a hundred times and knew exactly how to give each other what we wanted in such a way that we could kiss like this forever yet never have it be enough.

I had kissed a lot of guys in my life—way more than I'd ever want to admit. But kissing this man— Incognito or whoever he was beneath the mask—was one of the best kisses I'd ever had.

"This is crazy." He sighed when his lips returned to my mouth. "This wasn't supposed to happen."

"I know," I said, letting out a sigh before kissing him again.

And as his lips wove a spell over my mind, I decided not to think anymore. I was simply going to let myself feel everything there was to feel in this unbelievable moment.

Minutes passed, and even though I wanted to keep kissing Incognito forever, I knew if we didn't open that door soon, Miranda would probably return and find us once again in a compromising position.

"I should probably go," I said, pulling away, my chest heaving from the past few minutes.

"I know," he said, resting his forehead against mine and sounding like he was just as out of breath as I was. "But before you go, there's just one more birthday present I want to give you."

"There is?" I asked, having no idea what else he could have to give me.

"Yes," he said. "There's just one thing I have to do first."

And before I could ask what, he stepped away from me for a moment and flipped the light switch off that controlled the lamps, immersing us in pitch blackness.

What was he going to do?

Normally, I would feel uneasy about suddenly being plunged into darkness with a man I had only just met. But I didn't feel that way with him. Even if I didn't know his real name, or what he really looked like, I knew Incognito was a good person. And even though it didn't make sense for me to trust someone I just met, I knew I could trust him. It was just something I felt deep in my bones.

His hand brushed against my shoulder a second later, like he was trying to feel his way around the dark room to get back to me. And when he seemed to realize that he'd found me, he said, "There you are," and gave my shoulder a gentle squeeze before letting his fingers trace their way down my arm until he was holding my hand in his.

He stepped forward so the toes of his shoes were next to mine, and I heard him sigh. "Meeting you here tonight, Maya, has been amazing," he said. "You are an incredible girl."

I nodded, even though he couldn't see me. "It's been pretty incredible for me, too."

Of all the nights I've had in my now twenty-eight years of life, this was hands down in the top five...if not the number one.

"I'm glad to hear it," he said. "I never want to be a disappointment."

Did he really think that was possible?

"You could never disappoint me," I said.

"I hope that's true," he said. "Because after tonight, I know it's going to be impossible to forget about you."

90

My whole insides turned to mush with his words. This guy could probably have any girl he wanted and here he was saying those words to me.

It was unbelievable.

Nonsensical.

But even my skepticism couldn't deny the sincerity in his voice.

He let go of my hand, and a second later, a rustling sound came from just in front of me where I imagined his head would be.

Then he stepped closer, and I felt the warmth of what I could only imagine was his cheek next to mine as he whispered in my ear, "Happy birthday, Maya." Then he slipped something into my hand, pressed a kiss on my cheek, and said, "I'll be in touch."

And before my brain could catch on to the fact that this was his way of saying goodbye, he stepped away and disappeared through the door.

I saw his silhouette through the crack of light that came from the hallway for only a second before the door shut again, leaving me alone in the pitch blackness of the room.

I groped around the wall for the light switch so I could flick the lamps back on and see what he'd put in my hand. The item was hard but thin—one side smooth, the other side rough with a sandpaper feel.

I flipped the switch on, and when my eyes adjusted to the light, I found myself looking at the black-and-gold mask I'd been gazing at all night.

He'd left me with his mask.

Which meant he was currently walking around The Colosseum under his true identity.

I hurried to open the door, hoping if I was fast enough I might catch a glimpse of him. But when I stepped into the hall, there was only Miranda and another male security guard standing there.

Incognito had disappeared into thin air.

CHAPTER NINE

THE NEXT WEEK WAS A BLUR. Summers at the floral shop were always busy with the orders I had to put together for all the weddings happening in my small town. But being busy was good. It helped the time pass by quickly. And arranging one center-piece after another—something I could almost do in my sleep—left my mind free to daydream about what would be happening on Saturday night.

Incognito hadn't left me with a phone number, and I hadn't had a chance to give him mine, so after he'd disappeared, I worried that would be the last I'd ever hear from him and that his talk of meeting up had just been talk.

But then on Tuesday afternoon, I received a text from his manager who must have gotten my number from Emma. His manager asked if I would be okay meeting Incognito at seven o'clock on Saturday.

Of course I said I could definitely meet him. Then they said to meet Incognito at the famous bridge on the outskirts of Maplebridge for a picnic.

I didn't know how I managed to get any sleep all week, since I'd been so jittery over the fact that he was actually coming to see me—that I hadn't imagined everything after all. But in just over twenty-four hours, I would be with Incognito again. And I would find out if that amazing kiss we'd shared had really meant anything to him.

Because I hadn't been able to stop thinking about it.

Would he reveal his true identity to me when we meet? I had no idea. I suspected it probably wouldn't be happening though, since we barely knew each other. But a small part of me hoped he would. Because I would love to have a face to finally put with the man who had practically turned my whole world upside down in a single night.

The bell on the floral shop's door rang as I was working on an arrangement of pink peonies. I looked up to see who would be coming in just five minutes before closing time and found Landon strolling in with his skateboard under his arm, his auburn hair windblown.

"Hey Landon." I smiled, happy to see him again. "What brings you here?"

He glanced around the room at the various flowers I had displayed on bookshelves, tables, and the floor. "I was on my way home from the university, saw your Jetta parked out front, and decided to stop by."

"Well, this is a pleasant surprise," I said. I hadn't seen him all week, which was pretty normal since I usually only ran into him when I was over at my parents' house. But considering how much he'd teased me about my meeting with Incognito last weekend, I had kind of expected for him to at least text me to ask how it went. "Have you been busy getting everything ready for your classes to start up in a couple of weeks?"

"I've been trying to." He set his skateboard on the floor, leaning it against the counter I was working at. "I'm teaching a new class this year, so it's taking more time to prepare than I've expected."

"Yeah?" I asked. "Still a psychology class, though, right? It's not like you're branching out into the art of skateboarding or some random music class, are you?"

"Music class?" He raised an eyebrow. "Yeah, not sure anyone would benefit much from that."

"You don't have a secret musical talent?" I raised an eyebrow. "No garage band I never heard about?"

"Not quite." He chuckled.

I grabbed a peony from the bucket next to me. "So what is this new class about?"

He leaned a hip against the counter. "It's a positive psychology class."

"Well, that sounds right up your alley," I said, remembering conversations we'd had in the past where he'd talk about trying to convince the psychology department to let him teach a class that focused more on the habits of happy people instead of those with mental disorders.

"I'm really excited about it. I think it's going to be my favorite class to teach this year."

"That's awesome." I smiled. "It's always great when you love your work."

"It is." He nodded. "I mean, it's not as glamorous as being a famous rock star who has to hide his face behind a mask, but it's fulfilling for a regular guy like me." He winked.

My cheeks warmed. "Not everyone can be a rock star, I guess." I added the last peony to the arrangement and turned it in a circle to inspect my work.

"And not everyone can own the best floral shop in town." Landon grabbed a peony from the bucket and inspected it, the veins in his muscled and tanned forearms flexing as he turned the flower in his hand. "What kind of flower is this, anyway?" he asked.

"It's a peony," I said. "They're my favorite flower."

"Your favorite?" he asked, eyeing me with his deep brown eyes.

I nodded. "I just love how thick and lush they are. They grow really well here in the spring and early summer, so when I finally buy my own house I plan to have bushes of them all around my yard."

"You don't get sick of being around them all day?"

I shook my head. "Never."

He set the peony back in the bucket. "Well, that's good. Because you definitely have a talent."

"Thank you," I said, my chest warming at his compliment. "I may not have a PhD like you, but I do love my work."

And deciding that the arrangement I'd made for Reagan Adam's wedding did indeed look complete, I carried it to one of the fridges along the wall to sit with the other fifteen I'd made for the centerpieces.

When I returned to the counter, Landon asked,

"How much longer until you close up shop for the day?"

I looked at the clock. "I just have a few things to take care of and I'll be done. So probably fifteen minutes."

"Well, if you don't have plans already, I'd love to hear all about your meeting with the infamous Incognito."

And there it was. He was interested in hearing about it after all.

A slow smile spread across my lips. "I'll only spill the beans if food is involved."

"Is the Maplebridge Grill still your favorite burger place?" He raised a dark eyebrow.

I was surprised he remembered. I didn't think we'd been there together since college. "Their Old-fashioned Burger and strawberry shakes are the best."

"I might have to disagree and say that their Porky Bacon Burger is actually the best—but how about I help you clean up and we call it a date?"

CHAPTER TEN

LANDON SWEPT the floor while I took care of the cash register, and within fifteen minutes we were driving in my Jetta toward the Maplebridge Grill.

We got our food to go and then headed to the Canyon Park to eat by the little stream that ran through the park.

"So you never did respond to my last text, you know?" Landon said, settling into the spot on the grass next to me and taking off his shoes to put his feet in the cold water.

"You texted me?" I furrowed my brow.

He nodded. "It probably came through while you were talking to your famous lover boy, so it's okay if you missed it."

"Oh!" My cheeks flamed as I remembered the text he was talking about.

"What?" He cocked his head to the side and studied my face. "So you got it after all and were just ignoring me?"

"I'll say that I got it." I shook my head. "In fact, Incognito saw it, too."

"He did?" Landon's eyes widened. But somehow he didn't seem as surprised as I thought he should.

"Yeah."

"And?" Landon gestured with his hand for me to continue.

"Well." I started pulling open the paper wrapping on my hamburger. "After feeling completely humiliated and, like, I should probably just run out of the room, it actually might have helped me in the end."

"You kissed him?" Landon's mouth dropped open.

I couldn't keep a huge smile from my lips as I remembered everything. "Apparently, it made him curious enough that when I kissed him, he didn't push me away."

"*You* actually kissed *him*?" Landon bit his lip and gave his head a slight shake, as if I'd shocked him in a good way. "Dang girl. You *are* bold."

"You practically dared me to, so I had to." I shrugged like it had been simple, even though I knew I was very lucky Incognito hadn't called security on me when I threw myself into his arms.

Landon leaned back on one of his hands to face me better. "More like you did it because *you* wanted to."

"So maybe I did."

"And?" Landon asked. "Do famous rock stars kiss better than psychology professors?"

"I don't know." I looked down at my burger in my lap, suddenly shy for some reason.

"You don't have to worry about hurting my feelings. I just want to know."

But that was just the thing. I really didn't know. I'd kissed Landon two months ago, and even though so much time had passed, I still got butterflies in my stomach whenever I thought about it.

So that told me it had been really good.

But the kiss with Incognito had been amazing, too, and I was sure that two months from now I would still feel the same.

I pressed my lips together as I looked up at Landon, and when I gazed at his mouth I briefly wondered what he would look like with a mask on his face. A black-and-gold masquerade mask like the one currently sitting on my bedroom dresser, to be precise.

For a crazy moment, my mind twisted the image so much that his and Incognito's mouth and jawline looked the same.

But it couldn't be possible.

Sure, they both had strong jaws and both guys were amazing kissers, but Incognito's eyes were very blue and while Landon's eyes had as much life sparking in them as Incognito's had, his were dark brown.

Landon and Incognito could not be the same guy.

And even though that would make my confusing feelings so much easier to handle—if they were one person instead of two different guys who made me feel amazing when I was around them—I knew it was impossible.

I mean, it would totally be fun to date a guy who was a cool, skateboarding psychology professor by day and a make-your-heart-stop-with-that-hypnotic-voice kind of rock star by night. But as cool as that would be, it was impossible.

"What?" Landon furrowed his brow and wiped at his chin when I'd stared at him for too long. "Did I get ketchup on my cheek or something?"

"No." I shook away my thoughts. "I, uh, I just zoned out for a minute."

Landon smirked as he lifted a fry to his perfectly shaped mouth. "Daydreaming about Incognito?"

I bit my bottom lip and urged my blush not to come. But of course my cheeks burned anyway, because lately, all I ever seemed to do around Landon was blush.

But since I didn't need Landon to know that he made me flustered more often than not, I pulled my shoulders back and in as confident a voice as I could muster in that moment, I said, "And to answer your question, I would have to say that rock stars have similar kissing abilities as psychology professors."

"Well..." He bit into another fry then looked back at me and sighed. "I'm sorry he was a disappointment."

I lifted my burger in my hands and said, "I never said he disappointed."

And when I looked sideways at Landon as I took a bite of my Old-fashioned Burger, the way he was fighting a smile told me he was more than pleased with himself.

CHAPTER ELEVEN

"SO IF YOU KISSED HIM, does that mean there are plans for you to see him again?" Landon asked as we put the wrappers and empty cups from our dinner in a garbage can by the park's pavilion.

"Actually," I said. "He's coming to Maplebridge tomorrow."

"Really?" Landon asked. "That must have been an epic kiss if he's coming all the way here to see you."

"Yeah, I don't know what to think actually," I said, the anxious pit that had been in my stomach off and on all week flaring up again at Landon's acknowledgment of just how unheard of something like this was.

"Do you want to walk and talk?" Landon

gestured to the asphalt bike trail that led out of the park and into the canyon just beyond.

"Sure," I said. Maybe Landon could help me figure things out. He was a psychology professor after all. He might have some expertise in the area.

So we walked up the little hill that led out of the park and onto the canyon trail, and I tried to figure out what I wanted to say to Landon to gain clarity.

"So what's got you feeling anxious about Incognito coming here tomorrow?" Landon asked after a group of cyclists passed us by. "Worried he'll like you so much that he'll swoop you away from Maplebridge and you'll never get to see your old friends like me again?" He glanced sideways at me and winked.

"No." I smiled, appreciating the fact that he was always able to lighten the mood when I needed it. "I definitely don't think I'm in danger of anything like that."

"Then are you worried because you think he's planning to take off his mask and you don't want to hurt his feelings with how loudly you scream?"

"Landon!" I said. "For the last time. He's not ugly."

Landon shrugged. "You keep saying it, but until I have actual photo evidence I simply can't believe it."

"I bet you'd be the first to unmask him if you saw him, huh?"

"Probably."

I shook my head. "Even if he wasn't that great to look at, I would probably still like him because his voice and personality are that amazing."

He laughed. "Okay, then."

We walked a few paces, but instead of continuing on the main walking trail, Landon took me down a dirt path that led to a little waterfall. He pushed a few branches out of the way so I could pass without getting scratched, and then we were side by side again.

"So if you're not worried about your obvious admiration changing for him, what are you worried about tomorrow?"

I pressed my lips together as I thought about it, trying to figure out how to word what I was feeling. Then I sighed and gave Landon a cautious look. "I guess I'm worried that I'm going to sabotage myself again."

"Sabotage yourself?" He furrowed his brow and studied my face. "What do you mean?"

"I don't know." I lifted my arms at my sides. "I guess it's just something I always do when things seem to be too good to be true. I stop myself from getting whatever I'm working toward right at the last minute, and then I do something to make sure I can't go back and fix it."

"Like calling off your wedding and then making out with me?" he asked in a quiet voice.

His simple question hit me like a ton of bricks, knocking the breath out of me. Because it was true.

It showed that even though I was twenty-eight years old, I still hadn't changed enough to allow myself to grow up and be an adult.

I didn't regret calling off the wedding because I knew Gavin and I really wouldn't have made each other happy in the end. But I should have done it differently. I shouldn't have waited so long to end things. And I shouldn't have tried to numb the pain by bringing Landon into my mess.

"I guess it's kind of like that." I swallowed and looked down at my feet as we walked along the dirt trail. "Do you think I'm a horrible person for what I did?"

"Not horrible," Landon was nice enough to say. "We all do things that we regret."

But that was just the thing. In that instance, I actually didn't regret any of what I'd done that night. In fact, even though Landon and I were still just friends and he obviously didn't have romantic feel-

ings for me like I had for him, I think I would probably always look back on that kiss with fondness.

And so just so that Landon wouldn't be under
the wrong impression of where my feelings were
regarding that night, I said, "I don't regret it."

He stopped in his tracks. When I stopped and
turned to look at him, his dark eyebrows were knitted
together and his eyes seemed to search mine. Like
my confession had shocked him. And when he kept
staring at me, I worried that maybe I shouldn't have
admitted what I did.

"You don't regret it?" he asked in a low voice.

"No." I tucked some hair behind my ear, feeling
like he could see more of me in that moment than I
wanted him to. "Do you think I should regret it?"

"No, of course not." He shook his head quickly.

"Then why are you looking at me like that?"

"Like what?"

"Like I'm a weird alien and you're trying to
figure out what to do with me."

Because even if he never had romantic feelings
toward me, I still wanted to stay friends. I didn't
want to have just made things really awkward
between us.

But he shook his head and chuckled. "I don't
think you're an alien."

"Then why are you looking at me like I am?" I whispered.

He pressed his lips together and stared at the ground for a moment, the toe of his Vans drawing a short line in the dirt. Then his brown eyes lifted back up to mine and he said, "I guess now I'm just wondering what might have happened if I hadn't left on my trip the next day."

Oh.

Would something have happened?

Would he have wanted to change our friendship into something more? Have more kisses like that?

My heart started racing as I thought about what he might say next.

He pushed his hands into his pockets and started walking again.

"Do you think something might have happened?" I stepped quickly to catch up to him.

"I don't know." He shrugged. "I mean, I probably would have offered to help you cancel all your wedding arrangements after that just to have a reason to spend time with you. And then once you'd had enough time to heal, I probably would have tried to find an excuse to kiss you again."

My heart stuttered to a stop, not believing what I was hearing. "Really?"

He stopped under a tall, shady tree and looked at me. "It was a great kiss, Maya." There was so much sincerity in his eyes that my insides started melting. "Maybe moments like that happen for you all the time. But for me..." He sighed and gazed off into the distance for a moment before meeting my eyes again. "That kind of thing doesn't happen all that often. Maybe never before."

The kiss had affected him that much?

I was still trying to figure out how to respond— deciding whether I should tell him that kind of kiss didn't happen all the time to me either. That it had only been with him and Incognito that I'd felt those kinds of fireworks.

But before I could figure out how to word my thoughts, he said, "But it's okay if you don't feel the same way. I know you have your thing with Incognito tomorrow and it's probably going to be amazing. And no girl that I know would choose a psychology professor when she could have a rock star."

I might have.

If I'd known it was even an option.

If Landon hadn't left on his trip and he'd told me all this two months ago before I even met and kissed Incognito, I never would have even been in this situation.

If things had gone differently and we'd become something more than friends, I would have brought Landon to the concert with me. And if I did still end up backstage with the masked rock star, I would have simply talked and fangirled a little over him before inevitably leaving to go back home to kiss the guy who had been by my side for the past twenty-three years.

Because even though I hadn't fully realized it until this moment, I'd always had a crush on Landon. Ever since I moved here and his five-year-old self had called me his honey, I had wanted him.

I just never thought he wanted someone like me. He'd never acted like he did, anyway.

Which made me wonder why he was even saying these things now.

Was he just trying to get in my head before I met with Incognito tomorrow because he didn't like him?

"If you really thought all those things you're saying, then why didn't you tell me a week ago when you got back?" I asked, feeling somewhat annoyed at him for even putting me in this situation in the first place. "Why not say something before, instead of telling me to kiss Incognito?"

Because if that kiss had really meant as much to

him as he was saying, he wouldn't have told me multiple times to kiss another guy.

At least, when I really wanted a guy to choose me, I didn't go tell them to kiss another girl.

"It just kind of feels like you're playing with my feelings right now, Landon," I said.

For what reason? I had no idea. Landon didn't seem like the kind of guy to mess with girls that way. Yes, he understood human psychology, but I didn't think he'd use it to play with people's emotions.

"It's complicated, Maya," was all he said, as if that explained everything.

I folded my arms across my chest. "It's complicated now," I said. "Now that I have a famous rock star flying all the way here from wherever he lives to see me... Until today, I only thought you ever wanted to be friends."

"I know. I have bad timing. And..." He blew out a long breath. "I just—" He shook his head. "I know everyone thinks that I don't date that much because I keep my schedule way too busy. But really, I keep myself busy and don't let anyone get close to me because I'm afraid that if I put myself out there and let someone in to see everything about me, they'll realize that I'm really not as cool as they think. I'm just a regular guy. Easily replaceable once a cooler, hotter, more talented guy shows up."

"So were you telling me to kiss Incognito as some sort of test?" I narrowed my eyes, feeling so confused at his thought process. "Like, were you hoping that it would go badly, and then I'd tell you that you kissed better than him and that we should get married now?"

"No." He shook his head. "That's not what I was thinking at all."

"Then why tell me tonight—the night before possibly one of the biggest nights of my life—that you wish you hadn't gone on your stupid two-month long road trip?"

He ran a hand through his hair. "Because you have always chosen the other guy, Maya." His voice came out more passionately than I expected. "Ever since kindergarten, you have always chosen every other guy before me. I watched you date guy after guy in high school. You dated my best friend. You dated college guys. You dated pretty much every guy on the football team, but me. The same thing happened in college. So excuse me if I was a little worried that history would repeat itself."

Okay. Now *I* was getting mad.

He was blaming his never telling me about his feelings on the fact that I dated other guys?

"Yes, I dated a lot of guys." I stepped closer to him, adrenaline rushing through my body because I was frustrated that he could be so frustrated. "They asked me out and I said yes. And sure, I ended up dating a few of them. That's what you're supposed to do when you're young: date people, have fun, and figure out what you like." I lifted up my hands. "You're acting like I purposely dated everyone besides you. But did you even like me back then? Did you ever try asking me out? Because until about two minutes ago, I thought you only ever saw me as the girl you grew up next door to. A girl who you sometimes had fun flirting with, and yes, had that epic kiss with at the beginning of the summer. But you never once gave me any indication that you wanted me enough to try to actually pursue me."

"I thought it was obvious." He frowned, and his chest rose and fell like he was suddenly out of breath. "Every time you looked at me across the fence when I was mowing my lawn, every time our eyes locked when we said an inside joke in front of our friends, every time we were supposed to be doing homework but instead sent messages to each other through our bedroom windows, I thought it was obvious. Obvious that I was crushing on you so hard I couldn't even think about anyone else."

I frowned, remembering all those moments he was talking about. "I thought that was just you flirting with me like you flirted with every other girl at school."

"It was different."

"Different?" I blew out a breath. "If you felt that way, then why didn't you ask me out?"

"Because every time I finally got up the nerve, I found out you were already dating someone new. I was always a day late and a dollar short."

I had dated a lot back then. I'd lost track of how many boyfriends I'd had before I even graduated high school. But it still couldn't be all my fault that nothing had ever happened between us.

"Even if I went through guys faster than a newborn goes through bottles, you still should have tried," I said. "Then I would have at least known it was even an option."

He stepped closer, so there were only a few inches between us, took my hands in his and rested his forehead against mine. "So you're saying that if I had asked you out, you would have said yes?"

"Of course, Landon," I said, searching his eyes and hoping he was truly being sincere in everything he was saying and wasn't about to mock me and my own insecurities. "You were always way cooler than any of the guys I went out with. I just never thought I was cool enough to ever have a chance with you."

He just stood there for a moment, running his thumbs across the back of my knuckles before saying, "And if I'd tried to kiss you way back then, you would have let me?"

His gaze fell to my lips, and I licked them, anticipation filling my veins.

"Yes."

Before I could do or say anything else, Landon was tangling his fingers in my hair and kissing me. He kissed me again and again, and I kissed him back. And even though I hadn't known the depth of his feelings until tonight, or even really understood my own, I felt years of misunderstandings, heartache, and longing unravel as we kissed.

His hands moved from my hair, tracing their way down to my waist and pulling me even closer to him. My heart raced as I ran my fingers across his shoulders, feeling his tightly corded muscles and loving the feel of his strong body next to mine. We'd been sitting the last time we kissed, so being able to be so close to him right now felt amazing—yet somehow familiar, like he'd held me against him like this before. And even though it had been two months since we'd kissed, we fell into an easy rhythm that I usually only felt after kissing a guy multiple times.

Kind of like the kiss with Incognito.

No...

I pushed the thought away. I didn't want to think about kissing Incognito right now. I didn't want to worry about him because I just wanted to experience *this* moment. This beautiful and amazing moment with a guy who had secretly wanted me for years.

I'd always wanted someone who would care about me that much. For all the brevity of my previous relationships, I'd always wanted someone steady and unwavering who would stick with me no matter what. And that was exactly what Landon had done.

So many years had gone by, and even though he'd moved away from Maplebridge for a few years to get his master's and PhD, he had always come back. And we'd always been able to pick up our friendship from where it had left off.

Weren't the most successful relationships built with someone who not only lit your world on fire, but also was just a really great friend? Because if you were true friends, who really just enjoyed being with the other person, you could work through the hard things together.

Which told me this thing with Landon had much higher chances of working out than any fleeting fling I might have had with Incognito.

I had been infatuated with Incognito. But I still didn't know very much about him besides the fact that his accent was fake and he was an amazing musician.

But I knew Landon. Knew all the little details that you learned about someone after twenty-three years.

And I knew that if I didn't screw things up, we could be amazing.

Our kiss slowed and deepened. Landon's lips became gentle, tasting of mint and desire. He pulled me against the tree, pushing his body so close against mine that there was no space left between us.

As his lips wove a magic spell over my mind, it showed me the depth of his feelings. I knew, instinctively, that he wanted me as much as I wanted him in that moment.

After thoroughly causing chills to course through my body and fire to burn in my veins, he rested his forehead against mine, his breathing ragged.

As we both tried to catch our breath, I studied

his handsome face, his strong jaw, his deep, brown eyes. I inhaled the scent of his delicious aftershave.

He was everything I ever wanted but never thought I could have. He might have said that a psychology professor couldn't compare to a famous rock star, but he was more special than any famous celebrity could ever be. Because he was real. And he was here. And as long as I didn't mess anything up, I had a feeling that he could be mine.

Forever.

"We should have done this a long time ago," Landon said in a husky voice that made butterflies take flight in my stomach.

"I know," I whispered. "I never should have chosen Tyler Velario over you in kindergarten."

"I can't argue with that." Landon chuckled, a deep throaty sound and then we were kissing again.

I didn't know how long we stayed under that tree kissing, but the sun had started to dip behind the mountains before we finally came up for air.

Landon pulled away first and placed my head against his chest, his chin resting on the top of my head. "We should probably get back to your car," he mumbled lazily. "Before some little kid comes wandering down this secret trail and finds us."

"Okay," I said with a sigh, even though untangling myself from his arms was about the last thing I wanted to do. I tilted my head back and kissed his cheek one more time. "But I'm only going to agree to driving you home if you promise not to wait another two months before you kiss me like that."

He got a huge smile on his face. "Oh, I'm pretty sure that won't be a problem."

CHAPTER TWELVE

"SO WHAT ARE you going to tell Incognito?" Landon asked when I parked in front of his house a while later. "Did what happened at the park change anything for you?"

"Change anything" would be an understatement.

But even though I was over the moon with the sudden changes between Landon and me, it didn't make me feel any less sick about what I was going to have to do tomorrow.

"What do you think I should do?" I asked. Because for all I knew, Incognito could already be in Maplebridge, getting ready for whatever he had planned for our picnic tomorrow. And that would make cancelling this picnic a whole lot like what I'd done two months ago when I cancelled my wedding at the last minute.

Was I ever going to stop having these "Sorry, Maya changed her mind" moments?

Landon scratched at his cuticle with this thumb. "I'm not going to tell you not to go if that's what you're asking me to do."

"You're not?" I frowned.

Because after what we'd just experienced tonight, it kind of seemed like the thing a guy who wanted a relationship with me would do.

"Not that I *want* you to see him," Landon said, making my anxiety dissipate a little. "I'm just not going to be the kind of guy who tells you what you can or can't do."

"So you'd be totally relaxed and chill about me meeting in the woods with a famous rock star that you already know I kissed and had great chemistry with?" I asked, testing him in a way.

He leaned over the arm rest between us so his face was inches away from mine. With a wicked smile on his lips, he said, "If that's how it is, then I would definitely make sure to remind you of just how much chemistry *we* have together." A devilish glint formed in his eyes. "Because, honey, with what

I have planned for you and me, you haven't experienced *anything* yet."

And even though I'd just been kissing him twenty minutes ago, my stomach muscles clenched tight with his words and I wanted nothing more than to find out what he was talking about.

Because daaaang, Landon could turn up the charm when he wanted.

How had I been missing out on this side of him for so long?

I licked my lips and when I spoke, my voice was shaky. "I-I'm pretty sure I'm totally down for all of that."

He grinned and briefly kissed my lips. "Then how about you come inside so I can show you something?"

Wait. What?

I furrowed my brow, my heart pounding like crazy. "Are you inviting me in to...?" My words trailed off because I was too embarrassed to say it.

I mean, I loved making out and pushing boundaries as much as the next girl, but I wasn't expecting to go from zero to a thousand all in one night.

Not when I just barely found out tonight there was even a chance with him.

Landon must have seen the anxiety in my face

because he laughed lightly and said, "It's not what you're thinking." He ran a thumb over my cheek and looked deeply into my eyes. "Because as much as I'm sure I would love that—and yeah, might be hoping for something like that in the future—I'm all about savoring each step in a relationship." He dropped his hand from my cheek and unbuckled his seatbelt. "But with that said, there's something I've been trying to figure out how to tell you for a while, and I think the best way to do that is to show you something in my basement."

Show me something in his basement?

I narrowed my eyes. "You don't have, like, creepy dolls or dead bodies down there, do you?"

"No dead bodies, dolls, or even weird torture rooms." He laughed. "It's a good surprise. At least, I think you will like it."

"Okay." So I turned off my car and followed him into his house.

LANDON FLICKED the lights on when we got inside and led me through the living room I'd spent many hours playing in with him as a kid. It had been renovated since his parents had owned the house—everything was very modern and sleek-looking now.

"Did you design this yourself?" I asked, wondering if renovating homes was one of his extra hobbies that kept him so busy.

But he shook his head and said, "Nah, I hired someone to redo and update the place. Do you like it?" He raised an eyebrow.

"I love it," I said. "It's beautiful."

Gorgeous, really.

The light color palate was so soothing I instantly felt at home in his space.

It was also much cleaner than I imagined a bachelor pad would be, too. Most guys I dated didn't know how to put their dirty socks away, so seeing that he was a good housekeeper earned him brownie points with me.

He led me around the light gray couch in the center of the room to the stairway that led to the basement.

"Like I said in the car, the surprise will be downstairs," he said. "So go ahead and head down there. I just need to run to my room real quick to get something."

"No torture rooms, right?" I asked.

He shook his head and smiled. "There's a heavily padded room, but no torture rooms."

A padded room?

He was a psychologist...did he have some sort of private practice that required a padded room?

"I promise, it's a good surprise," he said again. "I'll meet you down there in a few minutes."

When he turned to head toward the hall that led to the master bedroom, I grabbed the wood railing on the wall and made my way downstairs.

At the bottom of the stairs was a family room like I'd expected since I'd hung out down here lots of times when Landon threw parties in high school. And just outside the family room was a hall that led to a bathroom and three bedrooms.

Since he had piqued my interest with his mention of a padded room, I decided to take a quick peek in the bedrooms to see if I could figure out what he'd been talking about.

The first door led into a regular-looking bedroom. A queen-sized bed sat along the far wall with a nice dresser and nightstand set nearby.

I closed that door again and went to the second room. It had a rack of weights, a treadmill, and other workout equipment.

Well, now I knew how he stayed so ripped all the time.

I left his home gym and went to the last door at the end of the hall. And when I opened the door, I found the room he had been talking about.

Though it was definitely not the white padded room I had pictured in my head. Instead, the walls were covered with some sort of foam acoustic wall panels. And all along one section was a huge table with lots of really high tech-looking equipment.

I frowned as I looked at the various computer screens and the switch board. There was a big soundproofed vocal booth with multiple high end microphones sitting just outside it. And on another side of the room was a keyboard and various expensive-looking guitars.

What the heck?

I walked up to the guitars, and when my eyes caught on a very familiar-looking Gibson SG, the memory of Incognito standing on stage playing the complicated guitar solo in his song "Here I Am" came to mind.

And as I looked at the platinum records framed on the walls and the two Grammys sitting on a shelf, a million other details flooded through my mind, sending chills racing down my spine as I pieced everything together.

How had I never considered this before?

Because now that I saw all of this, it should have been obvious from the moment I stepped into that backstage room with Incognito that he was someone I already knew. Someone I'd known for a lifetime.

Because *Landon* was Incognito.

"I see you found my padded room," a familiar Australian-accented voice said from behind me, sending more chills racing down my spine.

And when I turned around, my heart leapt into my throat at the sight of a tall man with broad shoulders, wearing the same blue t-shirt and shorts Landon had been wearing earlier but with Incognito's blue eyes and what must be a spare black-and-gold masquerade mask covering his face.

"Y-you're Incognito?" I gasped, my brain swirling with so many thoughts.

How had he kept this secret for so long? Because I had zero clue until a few seconds ago that he was the rock star he had teased me relentlessly about.

He nodded. In his regular voice, he said, "Yes, Maya. It's me."

"Why didn't you tell me?" I just stared at him, so much confusion filling me. "We met, and I told you all those things and we played that game, and then we kissed...and you still didn't tell me?"

I didn't know how to feel. Should I feel betrayed? Mad? Happy?

I must have seemed so stupid. So blind.

"I wanted to tell you." He held his hands out at his sides in a helpless gesture. "I wanted to let you know the guy you were fangirling over was me. But every time I thought about taking off my mask and taking out my contacts, I kept imagining you being so disappointed that it was me and I just couldn't do it. I didn't want to ruin the fantasy for you." He sighed and his blue eyes searched mine with a vulnerability I hadn't expected. "I mean, there I was, sitting in the room with the girl I'd been in love with my whole life and she was finally wanting me the way I've always wanted her to want me. I didn't want to ruin the magic by letting you know it was me."

"But I would have loved that," I said. "After what happened tonight, isn't that obvious?"

"It's more obvious now." He rubbed a hand across the back of his neck, his bicep bulging with the movement. "But I didn't know that then. For all I knew, you'd go running out the door the moment I took off my mask and never be able to stomach listening to one of my songs again."

I stepped closer until we were only a few inches apart, and then I reached up to carefully slip the mask off his face.

It was a little strange to see the face I'd grown up with to have blue eyes instead of brown, but I couldn't help but smile as I looked at him because he was so, so handsome either way.

I ran my thumb along his cheek bone and he leaned his head into my hand.

"I told you Incognito couldn't be ugly under this mask," I whispered.

"You're not disappointed?" he asked, his eyes searching mine as if he still wasn't quite sure that I was attracted to him.

So I let my hands trail down his strong chest, slip them down his sides, and then wrapped my arms around his waist. "I'm pretty sure you might just be the hottest rock star I've ever seen."

And that earned me a small smile. "Are you sure?"

"Oh yeah." I nodded, a grin stretching wide on my face. "I'm actually kind of thankful that you wear the mask now, because if your fans knew what you really looked like, they would be even more rabid and would try all sorts of crazy things to steal you from me."

He laughed. "So you're claiming me as yours then?"

"Pretty sure you're stuck with me now, Landon." I nodded. "I am, after all, your number one fan, right?"

"You did say that you were." He wrapped his arms around me, pulled me close, and kissed the top of my head. "And since you're still my number one fan, I think it's about time I show you a song that I wrote about this girl I grew up with but never thought I had a chance with."

"You wrote a song about me?"

"Yeah...I did." And when he said that, he blushed in the most adorable way.

Gosh, he was so cute when he was bashful!

He stepped away from me and went to grab his acoustic guitar from its stand. Then he pulled me into the family room so we could sit on the couch together.

"Do you want me to wear the mask for the full effect?" he asked, glancing at the mask that I still held in my hands.

I shook my head. "If you don't mind, I'd love to hear it just from you."

"Okay," he said. Turning away for a moment, he removed the blue contacts from his eyes, set them on the coffee table in front of us, and then turned back to me, looking like his old self.

Then he lifted his guitar into position and started playing the intro to his song.

But as he started to play the chords, the song wasn't an unfamiliar one like I expected. Instead, I recognized it as the song that I had listened to on repeat for the first couple of months after it came out.

He was playing "Miles Away Next to You."

When his smooth voice with a raspy edge started singing about a guy who had loved a girl for a long time but felt like she was miles away because she didn't see him the way he wanted her to, my heart swelled up so big I thought it might burst.

This song had always been special to me, because I'd always dreamed of a guy wanting me the way the guy in the song wanted the girl.

When Landon met my gaze and gave me a wistful smile as he sang the chorus, I couldn't keep tears from coming to my eyes because of how much love I felt from him in that moment.

He had seen me all along. He'd never thought I was too crazy, or too impulsive, or too quirky.

He'd *liked* those things about me.

He'd wanted me despite all my flaws. I'd just been too oblivious to see it.

I wiped at my eye and watched him serenade me through my tears.

He was so amazing. The kind of guy that I had always wanted but never thought I'd get. And when I thought about it all, I became a blubbering mess because I was so overwhelmed with the impossibility of someone like him wanting someone like me.

When he finished the song with one last long note that penetrated my soul with the rich texture of his voice, my chest squeezed so tight I couldn't breathe.

"You're crying." He set his guitar on the coffee table and studied me for a moment.

I nodded but couldn't say anything because I was too choked up to speak.

He scooted onto the cushion beside me and pulled me against him. With his cheek resting against my hair, he asked, "What's wrong? Should I have worn the mask?"

"No." I pushed his chest and chuckled despite my tears. "I just wish I'd figured it out sooner." I nuzzled my head closer to him. "Think of all the time we could have been together if I hadn't been so blind."

"We figured it out when we needed to." He combed his fingers through my hair in a soothing way. "Having it happen like this just makes this moment all the sweeter for me."

I tilted my head back to look at him. "So you don't think I'm incredibly stupid for not seeing what was right in front of my eyes this whole time?"

He shook his head. "I've always thought you were amazing, Maya. And if anything, I should have said something sooner."

He kissed me then, and it was so tender and sweet that I literally thought I might burst.

He loved me. This man, who could have any woman in the world, wanted me.

After he'd kissed me for a long, long time, we pulled away and I let my body relax against him, just listening to his steady heartbeat for a moment.

"Does this mean I get to call you my honey again?" Landon asked, his breath warm against my head.

I looked up at him with a smile, and just because it was tradition, I whispered, "I'm not your honey."

He chuckled, a deep sound that rumbled in his chest.

But then I sat up to meet his eyes and said, "I'm only joking, of course. Because I would love nothing more than for you to call me your honey any time you want."

EPILOGUE
ONE YEAR LATER

"THANK you for such a great night, Las Vegas!" Landon—or *Incognito* as the rest of the world knew him—spoke into the microphone at the Colosseum, with his guitar in hand. "I just have one final song for you before I go."

He started playing the intro to "Miles Away Next to You," earning a roar of applause from the crowd who loved his hit song every bit as much as I did.

"I don't know if I've ever publicly shared the story behind this song." His fingers continued strumming the chords as the applause died down. "But I actually wrote this for someone very special to me. We've known each other for most of our lives, but being the chicken that I was, I took way too long to get up the nerve to ask her out."

Several *awws* and sighs came from the crowd.

Yes, he could pretty much say anything and his fans would go crazy over him because they loved him so much.

I couldn't really blame them, could I? I still fangirled over him frequently.

"But," he continued after the crowd of mostly females stopped swooning long enough for him to speak again. "About a year ago, I finally stopped being a chicken and told her how I felt."

He glanced away from the audience to look back to where I stood just behind the curtains, where only he could see me. "I love you, honey," he said, looking at me through the eyeholes in his mask. "And I want you to know that you are every bit as important to me now as you were when I wrote this song—even more so. And I can't wait for what's next for us."

I put my hand to my chest and beamed at him, feeling the love I had for this amazing man swell so big inside me. He gave me one of those special heart-felt smiles that he reserved only for me before turning back to the crowd.

And after his fans had a complete come-apart as they realized that their beloved Incognito was off the market and their dreams of making him theirs—which I could relate to more than they could know—were dashed because some other woman had stolen his heart, Landon began singing the song that I could still listen to on repeat all day.

As he sang *my* song, I couldn't help but relive the memories we'd created over the past year together and the lifetime before that.

I had truly never been so happy before in my whole life. Loving and dating Landon was everything I had ever dreamed of and more. He made me feel special every day, and never ceased to amaze me with his dedication to putting me and our relationship first. He still kept himself busy teaching a couple of courses at the university during the week and writing and performing his music some weekends and two months in the summer, but not a day had gone by where we hadn't either been together or video-called each other.

For the past few weeks, I had joined him as he performed on the biggest stages in the western states, and to be a part of it had been magical. But tonight was his last concert of his US tour, and we were both excited to talk more about taking our relationship to the next level.

Yes, I, Maya Brown, the girl who sabotaged every

relationship she'd ever been in, was talking about *marriage* with the man who I loved more than anything in the whole world.

And I was so excited about it!

So freaking excited.

Turns out, you just have to find the right person to give your heart to and things will turn out better than you could ever imagine.

Landon finished the song—the last note still giving me chills like it did every time he sang it live—and after bowing and thanking the crowd again, he handed his guitar to one of the stagehands and pulled me into his arms to kiss me.

"You did so amazing tonight," I whispered after breaking away from the kiss.

"Thank you," he said, his breathing ragged from the performance and the kiss. "It's always better when you're here."

The stagehands helped to un-mic him, and once he was free to go, he took my hand in his strong one and pulled me with him backstage to the same room I'd met him in almost exactly a year ago.

He flicked on the lights when we stepped inside, and sitting on the coffee table across the way was a cheesecake that was nearly identical to the one we'd had on my birthday last year. A small pink and gold polka-dotted gift bag sat beside it.

"I know your birthday isn't until tomorrow," Landon said, pulling me over to the couch with him and sitting so we were close. "But I couldn't resist recreating one of the best nights of my life."

"You're amazing, you know that?" I said, smiling from ear to ear at his thoughtfulness.

He lifted a shoulder. "I did just have thousands of fans yelling and screaming my name...so I guess I kind of knew it." He shot me a wicked grin so I would know he was just joking. "But before I let my Incognito ego get too big, there's something I wanted to do before we try this cake."

"There is?" I asked, anticipation filling me.

He nodded. "I just haven't been able to decide if you'd rather have Incognito do it or me."

"I guess it depends on what it is," I said, feeling breathless over what I thought he might be getting at.

"It's kind of a big deal," he said. "And depending on what you say...it might just be one of the most important things I ever do."

My limbs went tingly at his words and it was hard to breathe. But I managed to say, "As much as I'm still Incognito's number one fan, I'm kind of way more in love with a guy named Landon Holloway. So maybe whatever you're doing should come from him."

"Good." He sighed, a half-smile playing on his lips. "I just wanted to make sure you didn't like me just because I'm rich and famous."

"As if." I gently shoved him in the shoulder. "You know I'm only with you because you're hot and we look good together in photos."

He laughed and stood from the couch. Then after removing his mask and contacts and setting them on the coffee table, he turned back to me looking like his handsome self.

And with only a hint of nerves in his brown eyes, he reached into the gift bag sitting next to the cheese-cake and pulled out a small, black velvet box.

The kind of box that could only hold one thing.

When Landon got down on one knee, I felt lightheaded.

He looked into my eyes, and with so much love and sincerity, he said, "Maya Elise Brown, I've loved you for as long as I can remember. When I think about the future that I want, you're front and center in every dream. I'm never more happy than when we are together and I'd love nothing more than to share our lives together, to have kids, to make a million memories and grow old together.

140

So..." He sighed. "I just have one question to ask you."

He opened the box to reveal the most beautiful diamond ring I'd ever seen. Then he looked at me in the way that always lit my nerves on fire.

"I was your first kiss all those years ago, and I want to be your last. Will you marry me?"

It took a moment for me to catch my breath, but once I could speak, I said, "Yes, Landon." My voice cracked from all the emotions I was feeling. "I would marry you a thousand times, yes." His face lit up with my words, and then we were hugging and kissing and crying happy tears. "I want to grow old and gray with you," I said in between kisses. "And have lots of little Incognito babies running around in masks."

He laughed. "Masks, really?"

"Maybe at least for Halloween?" I smiled up at him as sweetly as I could. "It's kind of been on my bucket list since I heard your first album."

"You've been planning to marry me for that long?" He gave me a skeptical look.

"I planned to marry *Incognito*," I said, patting him on the chest. "You were just an extra bonus."

He shook his head and laughed again. "Well,

guess if it's been on your bucket list for that long we might be able to do that for one Halloween."

"And this is exactly why I love you so much," I said.

Then before we could get carried away with all the plans for the future I couldn't wait to start, he took the ring from the box and slipped it on my finger.

"I love you, Maya," he said, pulling me into his arms again. "And I can't wait to cross off a million bucket list items with you."

DEAR READER,

Enjoyed *Stolen Kisses from a Rockstar*?

Make sure you stay in the loop!

Sign up for Judy's Newsletter.

Join the Corry Crew on Facebook!

Follow me on Instagram

Would you like to read another Judy Corry story but wonder what to try next?

You'll love how Kate and Drew got their second chance at love in Assisting the Billionaire Bachelor!

Thank you so much for taking a chance on Maya

and Landon's story! I've been wanting to write their love story ever since they appeared in my novel Protect My Heart, so finally having it in book form is amazing, and sharing it with you wonderful readers is even better.

If you enjoyed reading this book and have the time, I'd love to hear your thoughts in a brief, honest review.

Always grateful,
Judy Corry

STAY CONNECTED

Join my Newsletter: https://subscribepage.com/
judycorry

Join the Corry Crew on Facebook: https://www.
facebook.com/groups/judycorrycrew/

Follow me on Instagram: @judycorry

Also By Judy Corry

Rich and Famous Series:

Assisting My Brother's Best Friend (Kate and Drew)

Hollywood and Ivy (Ivy and Justin)

Her Football Star Ex (Emerson and Vincent)

Friend Zone to End Zone (Arianna and Cole)

Stolen Kisses from a Rock Star (Maya and Landon)

Eden Falls Academy Series:

The Charade (Ava and Carter)

The Facade (Cambrielle and Mack)

The Ruse (Elyse and Asher)

The Confidant (Scarlett and Hunter)

The Confession — (Nash and Kiara) — Coming 2023!

Ridgewater High Series:

When We Began (Cassie and Liam)

Meet Me There (Ashlyn and Luke)

Don't Forget Me (Eliana and Jess)

It Was Always You (Lexi and Noah)

My Second Chance (Juliette and Easton)

My Mistletoe Mix-Up (Raven and Logan)

Forever Yours (Alyssa and Jace)

Standalone YA

Protect My Heart (Emma and Arie)

Kissing The Boy Next Door (Lauren and Wes)

EXCERPT FROM PROTECT MY HEART
EMMA

Today marked day nine of my boy-cleanse. That's right—I'd made it more than a week without drooling over any of the hot guys at school. I should have won an award for having such amazing self-control, considering cute guys had once been my biggest weakness—addiction, really.

After my horrible summer, I had to come up with a plan. My first step was to wean myself off all thoughts of boys and dating them. Where daydreaming about guys during German class used to be my favorite pastime, it was now strictly off-limits, even if those foreign guys in the textbook did look like male models. Nope, no big blue eyes or knee-weakening smile would enchant me this school year. And as for getting butterflies in my stomach, they were definitely not a good sign—merely a warning that my defenses were low and that I needed to run in the opposite direction.

My best friend, Maya, thought my boy-cleanse was stupid, but that's only because she'd never caught her boyfriend making out with the girl he'd always said was just his *good friend*. I should have known things were too good to be true. Popular guys like Nick Bergstrom didn't go for regular choir nerds like me.

I'd thought since Nick graduated last year, I wouldn't have to see him again. But it appeared that even college freshmen needed food every once in a while. That was why I was ducking down behind the chest freezer in Lana's Supermarket on a Friday afternoon, peeking over the top as I waited for Nick to push his cart down another aisle.

I watched him carefully as he moved farther from my hiding place, hoping the whole stack of cereal boxes would land on his head. When Nick finally turned down the chip aisle, I dashed toward the bakery to grab a loaf of French bread, wishing for the thousandth time that I didn't have to run errands for my mom in order to use her car. I mean, shouldn't being the youngest child have some perks? But no, not with my parents anyway.

I was dropping the bread in my cart when I caught sight of a guy walking toward me. He was probably a year or two older and tall, with hair so dark it was almost black and arms that were sculpted to perfection. This guy wasn't just cute. He had "World's Most Beautiful Man" written all over him. Seriously, he put poor Hans from my German textbook to shame.

I straightened as he sauntered closer, and I finally came to my senses when he smiled at me. *Be cool,* I thought as I smiled back. He pulled a bag of whole-wheat English muffins off the shelf and studied the ingredient list.

Realizing I was dangerously close to breaking my nine-day streak of not ogling guys, I maneuvered around him and shuffled out of the bakery, whispering my mantra: *boy-cleanse, boy-cleanse, boy-cleanse.* With a safe distance between us, I peeked back for one last glimpse. I must have stared at his broad shoulders a moment too long, because my cart collided with something. I snapped out of my trance and watched in horror as bagels and muffins toppled to the ground, landing in a heap.

For one tempting moment, I considered leaving the mess and bolting. But my conscience kicked in at the last minute, and I scrambled to pick up the mess, hoping the guy wouldn't notice...somehow. I had just finished stuffing a few boxes of poppy-seed muffins on the shelf when I turned around to find the gorgeous stranger crouched down with five bags of blueberry bagels in his arms.

You have to be kidding me! My face burned hotter than a curling iron.

"Looks like the bagels decided to attack you today." He chuckled as he placed them on the bakery cart.

"Yeah, they just jumped out at me. I think they wanted to scare me or something." I laughed uncomfortably, wishing I could turn invisible. I should have run from the mess when I had the chance.

"Usually it's the paper towels that come at me, but I'll watch out for the baked goods from now on." He winked and bent over to pick up the last box of muffins. He was both funny *and* cute—a deadly combination. Thankfully, the butterflies in my stomach were sounding the alarm to retreat. I needed to get away before I did something stupid like ask for his number—or ask whether he'd marry me. I never dared do things like that normally, but in my weakened state I could already feel my crazy side coming out.

Before I lost my inhibitions, I simply said,

"Thanks for your help..." and waited for him to give me his name.

"Arie." He cleared his throat and held his hand out. "My name is Arie."

Ar-ee. Ar-ee drives a Ferrari. The rhyme zipped through my head out of habit. I shook his outstretched hand, noticing his firm handshake. "Nice to meet you, Arie. I'm Emma." I hoped my palm wasn't noticeably sweaty.

He nodded, let my hand drop, and stuffed his hand in his pockets. "I just have to ask..." He squinted and tilted his head to the side, a half smile on his lips. "Were you hiding from someone earlier? I'm new in town and need to know if there are certain people I should avoid."

I cringed. "You saw that?"

He nodded.

How much more embarrassing could this afternoon get? Maybe I should run into the paper-towel display and let it bury me.

"I saw my ex-boyfriend and panicked." I shrugged.

"Oh." Arie nodded, then lowered his voice. "I'm guessing it wasn't a better-off-as-friends thing, then?"

"Not quite. It's hard to stay friends after being cheated on." Why was I telling him all this?

He looked over my shoulder, pointed a finger, and whispered, "Is that him?"

"What? Where?" I snapped my head around. When I didn't spot Nick anywhere close, I glanced back at Arie, only to find him chuckling.

That was just what a super hot guy would do—make a joke at someone else's expense. Nick had done that, too. I may have thought this guy, Arie, was good-looking at first glance, but now I had come to my senses. I could totally tell he must've had plastic surgery or something. His face was a little too perfect. And those muscles...he must spend half the day at the gym to get them that way—just big enough to seduce unassuming girls but not too beefy. Some guys were so in love with themselves.

I huffed and gripped my cart full of groceries. "Good one," I said. "But just so you know, it wasn't because of my ex that I lost control of my cart. It was purely accidental." I squared my shoulders, trying to appear unfazed—difficult considering I was having one of those hot flashes my mom always complained about. "Anyway, I better get going. My ice cream is melting." I actually couldn't even remember whether I'd picked up the ice cream yet, but I needed to get out of there before I did something else stupid.

"It was nice to meet you, Emma." He smiled. "I

hope we'll run into each other again sometime." His eyes twinkled like he had some secret delight.

I nodded and angled toward the produce section. "I'll try to keep my cart under control next time."

Arie grinned. It would be a shame if I *accidentally* ran over his foot as I left.

ARIE

"Hey, rookie. How's your first day on the job?" The voice of my new supervisor, Jason, boomed through my phone's earpiece. I sat in my truck and waited for my new assignment, Emma Howard, to finish putting her groceries in the trunk of her silver Toyota Camry.

"This internship will be more entertaining than I thought. Are supermarket accidents a regular occurrence for her?"

"Not usually." Jason laughed.

"What about mood swings? You guys told me she's an easygoing girl, but she seemed like she couldn't make up her mind whether to be nice to me or annoyed."

"Well," Jason said. "From what we've observed

from a distance, she seemed fine. But we're not the ones right there up close."

"Looks like I get to be the one to discover the answer to my question, then," I mumbled into my phone as I watched Emma put her grocery cart away. I hadn't figured teenage girls out when I was in high school; why had I expected it would be easier a few years later?

Once Emma had backed out of her parking spot, I put my truck in gear. "She's on the move again," I said. "I'll check in soon."

"Let me know if you need anything," Jason said. "And try not to attract too many high school girls with that baby face of yours. Emma is our focus and the only one we need you to befriend."

"That shouldn't be an issue," I said. That's the last thing I needed—hormonal girls trying to distract me from doing my job. If I kept to the shadows this weekend, I could avoid any attention until I officially started school on Monday.

It was hard to imagine one girl would need this much surveillance. She was harmless. I almost felt bad, deceiving her the way I had.

But that was the nature of my work.

Secrecy was everything.

Being an undercover bodyguard for a teenage

girl definitely wasn't my dream job, but it would look good on my résumé. And I needed all the experience I could get if I wanted a shot at the Secret Service someday. My being here had been carefully orchestrated in preparation for the expected danger. If someone found out who I really was, it could ruin years of planning...and a lot of document forging to get me into the school in the first place. Not even the principal or teachers could know I was undercover. There could be absolutely no slip-ups.

I followed Emma back to her house and parked across the street at one of the houses Jason and Sophie owned. The night agent, Bruce, had just moved in a couple of months ago, which made it easy for him to keep an eye on her place all night.

Emma got out of her car, popped the trunk, and grabbed several grocery bags before walking into the two-story brick house. The homes here in Utah were a lot newer than the ones in my neighborhood back in Cortland, New York.

From what I'd been told, her house seemed like a calm and loving place. She lived there with two happily married parents. Her dad owned his CPA firm, and her mom was a homemaker who volunteered for a lot of community things. Her older brother and sister were out of the house, leading productive lives. Yep, everyone and everything in her life seemed to be perfect.

Just like everything in mine had *seemed* normal from the outside. But just like my family, hers had dangerous secrets of their own. And unlike her, I'd been able to get away from mine.

Even if I was about to pretend to be in high school again, I'd take it over the pitying looks of the well-meaning citizens of Cortland. Anything would be better than staying in a town where my dad was still considered the local hero.

Find out what happens next here: http://mybook.to/ProtectMyHeart

ABOUT THE AUTHOR

Judy Corry is the USA Today Bestselling Author of YA and Contemporary Romance. She writes romance because she can't get enough of the feeling of falling in love. She's known for writing heart-pounding kisses, endearing characters, and hard-won happily ever afters.

She lives in Southern Utah with the boy who took her to Prom, their four rambunctious children, two dogs and a cat. She's addicted to love stories, dark chocolate and notebooks.

Made in the USA
Monee, IL
09 April 2023

31615988R00100